SPECIAL MESSAGE TO READERS

THE ULVERSCROFT FOUNDATION
(registered UK charity number 264873)
was established to provide funds for research, diagnosis and treatment of eye diseases.
Examples of major projects funded by the Ulverscroft Foundation are:-

- The Children's Eye Unit at Moorfields Eye Hospital, London
- The Ulverscroft Children's Eye Unit at Great Ormond Street Hospital for Sick Children
- Funding research into eye diseases and treatment at the Department of Ophthalmology, University of Leicester
- The Ulverscroft Vision Research Group, Institute of Child Health
- Twin operating theatres at the Western Ophthalmic Clinic, London
- The Chair of Ophthalmology at the Royal Australian College of Ophthalmologists

You can help further the work of the Foundation by making a donation or leaving a legacy. Every contribution is gratefully received. If you would like to help support the Foundation or require further information, please contact:

THE ULVERSCROFT FOUNDATION
The Green, Bradgate Road, Anstey
Leicester LE7 7FU, England
Tel: (0116) 236 4325

website: www.foundation

THE ONE A MONTH MAN .

Thirty years ago, Oxford was a city of fear for female students, terrorized by a killer dubbed 'The One-A-Month Man' due to the ritualistic regularity of his crimes. Advances in DNA profiling since the time of the murders have identified Richard Pope, son of a US senator and now a frontline CIA operative, as the killer — and survivor Tina Marlowe finds herself in danger once more . . . The bad but brilliant detective Mike Lorenzo, exiled from Scotland Yard, is assigned to trace Tina before she is tracked down by her lethal enemy — just the challenge he needs to redeem himself . . .

MICHAEL LITCHFIELD

THE ONE A MONTH MAN

Complete and Unabridged

ULVERSCROFT
Leicester

First published in Great Britain in 2012 by
Robert Hale Limited
London

First Large Print Edition
published 2013
by arrangement with
Robert Hale Limited
London

A catalogue record for this book is available
from the British Library.

ISBN 978–1–4448–1716–4

Published by
F. A. Thorpe (Publishing)
Anstey, Leicestershire

Set by Words & Graphics Ltd.
Anstey, Leicestershire
Printed and bound in Great Britain by
T. J. International Ltd., Padstow, Cornwall

This book is printed on acid-free paper

11871735

For Joanne
For all the missed years

1

Cold cases give me the creeps, like ghosts. By definition, they belong to the past, often rooted in another generation, another life-time, before the wheel was invented and someone came along with a weird notion that the world was round. Certainly long before DNA profiling revolutionized crime-solving. They're off my radar. Please excuse my little indulgence in flippancy, but they leave me cold. Digging up old bones doesn't excite me. If it has to be done, it's a job for burned-out cops; for plodders teetering on the threshold of retirement, anxious not to catch a bullet before reaching that exclusive old boys' club of long sleep-ins and unhurried walks, morning and evening, with a plodding, arthritic dog.

But I wasn't burned out. Neither was I looking for a sleepy sinecure. I was being assigned to reviewing old, unsolved cases because I'd trodden on toes. Not big toes. I hadn't slept with the commissioner's wife, not even his mistress, which probably would have been a more unwise indiscretion than tampering with his spouse. Neither had I planted evidence to secure a wrongful conviction or taken a bribe to derail an investigation. I'd simply crawled up the nose of one of my superiors; a nasty, anti-social habit of mine. My punishment was to be shunted to the sin bin — my derogatory name for cold-case duties. Not even in London, although I'd been with the Met since the day, like a Boy Scout, I took some kind of mumbo-jumbo oath.

Exiling me to Oxford seemed like enforced deportation, tantamount to Napoleon's Elba. Not that I had anything personal against Oxford, but I'm a Londoner and in spirit I shall always be; from womb to tomb, plus that rather critical bit in the middle. London is my comfort zone. I understand its crime, its villains, its humour, its rhythms and tempo, plus its dark and light sides. London is the lung that pumps my oxygen and spurs my pulse. I breathe it. I hate the place, love it, and couldn't live without its rotten, smelly, polluted and pulsating beauty and ugliness.

My ambivalence towards London was shared by almost everyone I grew up with. Whenever an investigation took me away from the capital, I was always as excited as a boy going on holiday, but within a couple of days I would be pining for the chaos, the gridlock, my old haunts and the racing heartbeat. There was so much majesty in all the madness that was London. I itched for *my* pubs, *my* betting shops, *my* casinos, *my* restaurants, *my* whores, and *my* gangsters.

Of course, Oxford is a stunning city architecturally. It has its own personality. Some of my peers at Scotland Yard even completed their education there, among the dreaming spires and elite students. Me? My education was more basic. Truncated, you might say. I learned on the job. As a teenager, I ran with an East End gang. When I crossed over from poacher to gamekeeper, I became a cop on the beat — beating all the college-educated boys and girls through the ranks to detective inspector.

Unfortunately, my clashes with authority were as legendary as my innate flair for flushing out human parasites in the urban, labyrinthine sewer that would always be my Garden of Eden. So many rotten apples. So much succulent fruit that never failed to tempt. So much that I would never be able to resist. London had everything. Grief, it even had me!

Detective Superintendent Bill Sharkey had a florid face and a figure that reminded me of a jolly farmer who over-indulged on his own dairy products. His paunch made him appear deceptively shorter than he really was.

As we shook hands in Oxford's Central Police Station our eyes were level, so I knew that he must be a six-footer.

'So you've come to show us provincials how the job should be done, eh?' he said, mirthlessly, resentment flaring in his porcine eyes.

I wasn't the least surprised by this bigotry. There had always been hostility in the provinces towards the perceived elitism bred at Scotland Yard and throughout the Met. Sharkey's stereotype stance wasn't new to me by any means.

'It's my understanding that *you* asked for help,' I said, neutrally; a tone of boredom coming easily to my nicotine-tuned voice.

'*I* didn't ask for anything.' Sharkey's gravelly voice resembled a growl. 'The request came from my chief constable. No input from me.'

'Well, if I'm surplus to requirements, I'll happily hotfoot it back to my homeland, without wasting another minute of your precious time,' I said, cornering him. In a nutshell, I was saying, *put up or shut up*, and he knew it.

'Sit down, Lorenzo,' he said, all steam evaporated. As soon as I was sitting opposite him, across his desk, he asked gruffly, 'I suppose you know why you're here?'

'To work cold cases,' I said, not attempting to mask my lack of enthusiasm.

He leaned backwards, crossed his legs, and massaged his puffy lips with fingers almost as nicotine stained as mine. 'Not exactly,' he said. 'You're here to work *a* cold case — singular.'

It is with some shame that I have to admit I was suddenly vaguely intrigued as it filtered through that I wasn't there merely for an academic, box-ticking exercise, simply to meet government targets.

There was a buff folder on Sharkey's desk, which he now flicked open. 'Thirty years ago, three women were murdered in Oxford. Another woman was attacked, but managed to escape. We know that the same man was responsible for the four crimes.'

'How do you know?' I cut in.

'I'll explain if you shut up until I've finished,' he berated me.

No finesse with this fella. I was almost warming to him. My kind of animal. I reckoned he could bite as well as bark.

'The youngest of the victims was aged twenty; the oldest twenty-three. All four were students. Two of them were reading law.'

'And the other two?' I could never do as I was told, something that had consistently got me into trouble since my earliest schooldays, but Sharkey didn't snap this time. I think he appreciated the fact that I seemed hooked.

'Modern history and politics. The survivor was the twenty-year-old. She was the political student and the last of the four to be assaulted. All the crimes were compressed into a four-month period. The press dubbed the perpetrator 'The One-A-Month Man'. Catchy, albeit tabloidy.'

'Except you didn't catch him.' My mouth had a mind of its own. Restraining it was beyond my control; the cross I'd borne all my thirty-eight years.

'I was a raw rookie at the time,' Sharkey countered defensively. 'In uniform. Directing traffic. Between ourselves, the detectives' work on this one was shoddy — at best. We — the force, not me personally, you understand — took a lot of flak from the media and political snakes. Locally, the hunt for 'The One-A-Month Man' was front-page news every day. The national press kept it running, too. The nation seemed fixated by it and Oxford was a city in fear. The general feeling was that there was a madman, a psychotic, running loose. Residents, the press and politicians couldn't understand why he hadn't been caught after the first murder. Women — especially female students — were warned not to go out alone after dark, which was like asking dogs not to pee on trees. The suspense went on for weeks, months.'

'But *he* didn't strike again?' I said.

'Stopped just like *that*,' said Sharkey, snapping his podgy fingers.

'Probably because he'd come close to being collared,' I suggested.

'Almost certainly. Now let me give you an overview.'

It was story time. My sort of story. A mystery. A tantalizing whodunit. The fact that it was dated didn't matter any more. These crimes transcended datelines, the way Jack the Ripper had survived like a gnarled and twisted evergreen, growing bigger and more shadowy by the year. Murder by gaslight, for example, had a morbid, timeless fascination. Serial killers were never obsolete currency.

'The first murder was in September,' Sharkey began, ponderously, knowing he had a captive audience. 'The weather was still summery. Most of the university's students had just returned from their long summer break. But there was also a substantial new intake of freshers.' In the pedestrian manner of a tour guide with his pendulous features making me think he was more suited to the role of undertaker than crime-buster, he continued, 'Oxford is a very compact city.

'Now to the murders. In each case, the women had been drinking with friends. They were merrily drunk, but not legless, a fact garnered not just from those friends who had been with them, but also from blood analysis. Each victim had just ended a relationship. Bluntly, they'd just dumped boyfriends.'

'And were out celebrating their freedom?' I speculated.

'Sort of. None of the relationships appeared to have been serious, though. Just university romances, dating a few times, riverside pic-nics, pubbing . . . '

'And fucking,' I said, lowering the tone; my forte.

'Well, a bit of that, too, no doubt,' said Sharkey, not the least censorious. 'I'm not going to blitz you now with too much detail because it's all in there.' He poked the folder, which remained open in front of him, like a crib-sheet or TV autocue. 'The victims had been drinking most of the evening with a crowd of students, most from their own particular college.'

'An equal gender mix?' I wondered aloud.

'Roughly, as far as I can recall, but only a few were attached, as coupled.' Hastily, he added, 'By coupled, I mean emotionally, not necessarily physically, you understand.'

I understood, I assured him. 'I assume the

ex-boyfriends were interviewed?'

'Of course. Although I said the detective work was shoddy, it wasn't *that* bad.'

'And I take it they all had unshakable alibis?'

'Correct, as you'll see for yourself when you read the file. Even if they didn't have an alibi, it defied logic to imagine that any of them could be implicated.'

'Because none of the ex-boyfriends had ever dated more than one of the victims?' I said. Mischievously, I added, 'There was no cross-pollination? What about the crime locations and MO?' I asked.

'I was coming to those; in my own way and own time,' he said, irritably. 'Four different locations, but same MO. Let's focus first on number one, Louise Redman, because this is the template. As I've said, she was pubbing in a crowd. Suddenly, she had only a few minutes to get back to her college before lockup. So, like Cinderella, she made a run for it, barefooted, clutching her shoes, and waving goodbye to her friends, blowing kisses to all and sundry. The Turf Tavern, up an alley, is only a ten-minute bike dash from Lady Margaret Hall College.'

'But she didn't make it?' I said, needlessly.

'Her body was found next morning beside the River Cherwell, to the north of the city centre. Lady Margaret Hall is situated alongside the river.'

'Found by whom?'

'An early-morning dog walker, from the nearby Banbury Road, one of north Oxford's main drags. She was looking for some pancake-sized wild mushrooms in the dew, but came across more than she'd bargained for.'

'Was she clothed? Not the old dame, but Louise?'

'Fully.'

'No sexual assault? No rape?'

'Nope. Well, certainly no rape. Strangled with a nylon stocking. Not her own. Well, not one that she had been wearing. Forensics established that fibres embedded in her neck had come from a woman's nylon stocking.'

'Was the stocking ever traced?'

'No. But listen to this . . . ' He leaned across his desk like someone about to impart a never-to-be-repeated secret. 'A condom had been stuffed into her mouth. Not in its wrapping. Just one rubber.'

'A used condom?' I said, disgusted.

'No, that's the point, the strangest thing: a virgin condom, straight from the pack, it would seem.'

'Some calling card!' I remarked, carelessly.

'If it had been used, the semen would have

been a great lead, even in those primitive DNA days. The same MO was repeated in the next two murders; a virgin condom forced into the victim's mouth.'

'What about her bike? You said something about the pub being a ten-minute bike dash to the college. I guess that meant she had a bike outside the pub.'

'Her bike had been tossed into the river. It was fished out by frogmen searching for clues.'

'Any witnesses of worth?'

'Certainly not to the crime itself.'

'Any suggestion that she was followed from the pub?' I asked, mechanically.

'No evidence of that. If she was followed, the perp would have needed transport. Someone pedalling like fury on a bike behind her would have been a trifle obvious. Anyone in a car or motorbike would also have had difficulty remaining inconspicuous. More likely she came upon her killer near the college.'

'Someone waiting for her?'

'I doubt that he was waiting for her *specifically*. It was simply her unlucky night. If not her, it would have been some other unfortunate. Law of the lottery.'

'Random selection by an opportunist,' I said, for something to say.

11

'Someone out hunting,' said Sharkey. 'Someone who had gone out determined to make a kill. Just like Jack the Ripper, the Yorkshire Ripper, Ted Bundy and a host of others. Urban big-game hunters. Only one stipulation: the quarry had to be female and ripe.'

'But not for fucking, in this case,' I said, pensively; no disrespect intended for the dead.

'Don't be so sure.'

Now I *was* confused.

'Let's fast-forward the narrative to Number Four, Tina Marlowe, the survivor. Beginning of December. A cold, Friday night. Roads already icy by mid-evening. Starry, moonlit night. No cloud cover. Lots of student social activities. End of term approaching. Parties all over town. Sober concerts and boisterous knees-ups. By eight o'clock most of the students out on the town were already pissed.'

'And Tina Marlowe was one of the pissed?' I said, hoping to give the story a kick up the bum.

'She'd had a few, certainly.'

'Which pub?'

'The White Horse, between Blackwell's bookshop and Trinity College.'

'Was she a student of Trinity?'

'No, St Hilda's — another college on the bank of the Cherwell.'

'Any significance with the two colleges being beside the Cherwell?'

'No, Lady Margaret Hall is north of the city, whereas St Hilda's is south and on the opposite side of the river.'

'Could be someone with a motor-launch or houseboat, trawling the river fishing for females,' I said.

He pulled a face that revealed to me that this theory was one that hadn't been considered, but he didn't debate it — the reason for which I was soon to discover.

'Did any of the victims know one another?' I continued.

'One can't be a hundred per cent certain about that but apparently not. The only known links between the four is that they were all students on carefree nights out and separated themselves from the safety of numbers to become snapped up by a self-appointed, lurking Reaper. Tina was with two female friends and four male students. The lads, all from Trinity, knew about a party and were planning to gatecrash. They were chatting up the girls and trying to cajole them into tagging along. Tina's two friends agreed to go, but she had a headache developing and took a raincheck. She'd suffered from severe

13

classic migraine since childhood. Her vision was beginning to break up and she was seeing flashing lights. So she gave the party a miss. Said she'd better hit the sack as quickly as possible. One of the lads, who had wheels, offered to give her a lift to St Hilda's, but she declined, saying a walk in the cool air might blow away the woodpecker in her head.'

'Such trivial decisions so often choreograph destiny,' I observed, abstractly.

'If you say so,' he said, clearly not the philosophical type. 'Where was I?'

I'd irked him again by stemming his flow.

'Tina decided against partying,' I said, easing him back on track.

'That's right. She set out on foot from the pub. By this time there was a dusting of snow. She was wearing a duffel coat, scarf, woollen hat, sheepskin gloves, jeans and fur-lined boots. With her head buried inside the hood of her coat, she walked briskly, cutting through to the High from Broad Street, via Turl Street, which won't mean anything to you until you've studied a city-centre map or, better still, retraced the route she took, which was direct. Despite the weather, the pavements were heaving with pedestrian traffic, mostly students. All revellers, getting into the Christmas spirit, which tends to last year-round here. When Oxford swings, it's usually

14

good-natured. Not like from where you hail.'

I allowed the sniper's fire to pass overhead, as if unheard and missing its target.

'She crossed the High and headed past University College towards Magdalen Bridge. Now she was not far from her destination, barely five minutes away. The Botanic Gardens were on her right as she approached the bridge over the river. Not so many people about now, but plenty of cars and buses. Not a remote spot by any means. Halfway across the bridge she was overtaken by a male jogger. She thought he must be keen or bonkers; only a fanatic would be out running at that hour in snow. He was wearing a dark blue tracksuit; Oxford blue. She reckoned he was at least six feet tall. Well built, though she had only a rear view of him. He quickly drew clear of her, melting into the night. On the other side of the bridge is a roundabout, where Tina turned right, now just farting distance from her college. And that's when it happened.'

'The jogger was waiting for her?' I surmised.

'She had no idea where he came from, but suddenly he was behind her again, and this time he grabbed her around the neck and gagged her with a gloved hand. Despite feeling unwell and being overpowered and

15

outmatched, she fought like a tigress, kicking backwards and also managing to bite him through his woollen gloves, making him curse. 'Fucking bitch!' he swore, but not very loudly, almost under his breath. He spun her around so that she could see his face.'

'Full frontal?' I said, bemused. 'He wanted her to see his face? Intending it to be the last thing she'd see before dying?'

'Oh, yes. And how! His face, you see, was covered by a 'Scream' mask. She was petrified, naturally. As she prepared to turn to make a dash for her college, he said, 'Oh no you don't!' and punched her in the mouth, breaking four of her front teeth. Holding her by the shoulder with one hand, he pulled something from his trouser pocket. Any idea what it was?' he tested me.

'A condom,' I guessed.

'Right.' He looked mildly disappointed with my correct answer. ''This is for your Last Supper, after you've helped me fill it!' he said. And that's when she kicked him, with all the strength she could muster, in the bollocks. By then, he'd also pulled out a knife and a stocking. The kick winded him sufficiently to give her enough start to make it to St Hilda's before he got his breath back.'

'He didn't drop the knife or stocking?' I said.

'Unfortunately, no.'

'Any witnesses?'

'None.'

'Even though you said there were quite a few cars and buses around?'

'That was before she made the turn at the roundabout. However, there were clues. Firstly, she was positive that he spoke with a transatlantic accent; either American or Canadian. Voice experts collaborated with her for days, playing recordings of all the regional accents of the USA and Canada, but she couldn't narrow it down beyond his being North American. Nonetheless, that seemed a pretty useful lead.'

'Did she get a handle on his age?'

'In his twenties was the best she could do. He was athletic in stature, so the detectives initially working the case pencilled in the possibility that he was a student. With hindsight, the luckiest break for the investigation was the busting of Tina's mouth and the loss of her four front teeth.'

My curiosity must have been emblazoned across my face because he quickly elaborated.

'The teeth smashed from her mouth were recovered by scene-of-crime magpies. Those were the gnashers that had bitten through the attacker's gloves, drawing blood. Just a little. Just a few droplets, which the freezing temperature had frozen.'

'Have the teeth been preserved uncontaminated?' I asked eagerly.

'Oh, yes, but thirty years ago forensic science wasn't sufficiently advanced to help the detectives beyond determining blood group. Not very helpful because the blood group was the most common.'

'But put together with the Yankee voice, physical build, and age range, there was quite a bit to work with, I'd have thought,' I reasoned.

Sharkey showed no dissent. 'What went on three decades ago here is none of my business. It's history. My concern is what we do now. We have a second chance. We have to avoid a second cock-up. Lots of young men were pulled in for questioning. Their voices were taped and played to Tina.'

'Did they get any mileage from that angle?'

'A few potential candidates. For quite a time now, the US and Canada have been well represented among Oxford University's fraternity. But they all had alibis.'

'What about bite marks on a hand?'

'By the time the team had weeded out most of the North American students, all minor wounds would have healed, but hands were examined and one young man did have fading scars that could have been caused by teeth, a police doctor confirmed.'

'So there *was* a suspect?'

'Not for long. He was from Washington DC. A senator's son and rowing Blue. Richard Pope. Studying law. But really here just to row. An athletic import. His voice was played to Tina.'

'And?'

'She couldn't be sure.'

'What about his height and general physique?'

'Just about right, but Tina was too uncertain and wavering for her opinion to be anything near a positive ID. Anyhow, his alibi was enough to eliminate him. He was with his parents, who were staying at the Randolph Hotel that weekend. They were over for some pre-Christmas shopping. Richard Pope was into his third and final year.'

'At which college?'

'Balliol.'

'But he wasn't in residence the night of the attempted murder and/or rape of Tina Marlowe?'

'No, he dined with his parents at the Randolph and stayed with them overnight.'

'But not in the same bedroom?'

'No, he had an adjoining room, with a connecting door. They dined late.'

'Verified by staff?'

'Oh, yes. The maître d' remembered them,

mainly because of the generous tip he was given. After dining, they watched TV in the parents' room and were together around the time that Tina was turning into a vampire, sucking human blood from the bastard we've waited thirty years to ID.'

Something about Sharkey's last statement made my antennae flutter. 'So what's new thirty years on?'

'What's *new* is that we now have the identity of the 'One-A-Month Man'. Definite. Beyond all doubt.'

Now I really was getting a taste for this case. 'Who is it? Why hasn't he been arrested? Why do you need me?' My questions tumbled out like coins from a hole-riddled trouser pocket.

'A few more facts before I give you answers.'

He was determined to stretch the suspense.

'There was a road accident in London two months ago between a couple of cars. Both drivers were routinely breathalyzed. One was way over the limit. He was locked up for the night and charged. Before being released, a routine DNA sample was taken by swab.'

'And the DNA national profiling database came up trumps with a match,' I intervened, catching up. 'The blood from Tina's knocked-out teeth had come good after all those years.'

He didn't bother answering as he slid a little in his chair, appearing slumped, almost deflated, most certainly not high on an adrenaline surge, which seemed very contradictory behaviour in view of the apparent breakthrough. Why did so much seem skewed about this case? I was about to find out.

With fingers clasped against his triple chin and his lugubrious expression unmistakably hangdog, he said, 'It *was* Richard Pope, after all.'

A million questions stampeded from my head towards my mouth. I filtered and assembled them into orderly fashion as best I could.

'So his parents covered for him?'

Sharkey just shrugged.

'Where is he now?'

'In London.'

'Have you an address for him?'

'Oh, yeah. The US embassy.'

Our eyes locked as, for a few seconds, we communicated by silent transmission.

'He's a diplomat,' I speculated. 'And at the embassy he's on US soil, enjoying diplomatic immunity?'

'Immunity isn't an issue — *yet*,' said Sharkey. 'He's not aware we're on to him.'

'If a saliva sample was taken, even though it was thirty years ago, he'll remember, it'll be filed in his brain, and he'll know,' I persisted.

'He won't be aware of his blood on Tina's punched-out teeth; that was never made public. The media weren't even told that teeth had been knocked from Tina's mouth and taken away by forensics. That was one thing the lead detective did right. Throughout the investigation it was maintained that forensic harvesting had yielded bugger all.'

'What's his status at the embassy?'

'CIA branch.'

'Oh, shit!'

'But at the moment, he's the *least* of your problems.'

'*Your* problem, you mean?' I countered.

'No, *yours*,' he corrected me, his smile mean. 'From now on, it's all yours. That's the deal I cut with your commander. He hasn't much time for you, right?'

'He has when it suits him,' I mumbled, sulkily.

'But currently he's not suited.' Sharkey contrived a chuckle. 'However, he does say you're better than good. Possibly even the best ever — when you're off the juice, out of a betting shop, and not trespassing with your dick.'

'That sounds familiar rhetoric,' I said, sheepishly.

'I'm no moral gatekeeper, Inspector. What

22

you do socially is your own affair, within reason and as long as it doesn't impinge on your work. So I'm prepared to be philosophical and say Commander Dan Pomfrey's loss is my gain. OK?'

'Fair enough,' I said.

'Now to the problem . . . '

The theatrical pause that followed was finely tuned.

'Before you can bag the killer, you have to hunt down the victim. How's that for a twist?'

I'm sure the look on my face must have been equivalent to a sign that warned my brain had just fused and all lights were out.

The smile that slowly blossomed across the desk telegraphed confusing messages; it was partly patronizing, partly patriarchal. 'You see, we now know the ID of the 'One-A-Month Man'. We know where he is. But we haven't a clue where Tina Marlowe's living — or, indeed, if she is even still alive. If she is among the living, she's probably married and her name won't be Marlowe. She might be a grandmother by now. She could have emigrated after such a trauma. She could be anywhere on the planet — quite literally. But most importantly, she probably won't want to be found by you. We represent the dark side of her past, what she fled from; the skeleton in her cupboard. Her husband, children, in-laws and friends will almost certainly have been excluded from her secret. And one more thing: when she learns the identity of the man she'll be expected to testify against, she'll realize that, once again, she is in mortal danger. She can kill Pope's career, lifestyle, and future. She can embarrass the US government. She could conceivably be in more danger now than on that bleak winter's night thirty years ago. So, you see, you're as likely to be as unpopular with her as you will assuredly be with Pope.'

'The kind of cold case to get burned on,' I said.

'Pomfrey's very words,' Sharkey said, laughing.

2

Lunching alone at a historic restaurant in the High Street, I trolled through the file. Thirty years ago, Richard Pope was twenty-four years old, six feet and three inches tall, weighing thirteen stone. His complexion was described as fair, matching the mug-shot, eyes ice-blue. Hair black and cropped short. He had a strong, stubborn face with a square, pugilist's jaw. His build was said to be muscular: what else would you expect from a beefy Boat Race oarsman? The physical dimensions told me nothing about the man behind the mask. The 'Scream' mask.

Of course, there were no recent photos of him. The CIA weren't in the habit of circulating publicity shots of their operatives, especially if they were involved in *black ops*, such as trying to blow up dictators with explosive cigars or conspiring with gangsters to have presidents rubbed out; little party tricks like those.

Flicking backwards through the file, I came to his statement, made some three weeks after the assault on Tina Marlowe.

I was on the Thames in Oxford in the afternoon, while my parents shopped in London. I met them at the Randolph Hotel around five o'clock. We had afternoon tea; cakes and biscuits. We talked about mundane matters; what they'd bought in London, what we all wanted for Christmas, and where we'd dine that evening; those sorts of trivial things.

The weather was so miserable and cold, the three of us were in agreement that we'd stay in the hotel for dinner. Because we'd had a late afternoon-tea, we also decided that we'd eat late. After going to our rooms, I had a bath and lay on my bed, reading, watching some TV, and dozing.

Around seven-thirty, I had a shave and put on a suit for dinner. My parents are always particular about dressing formally when dining out. That's the way I've been brought up in Washington and I did it automatically wherever I was in the world — as did my parents, of course.

We had a couple of bottles of wine between the three of us with our meal and also a glass of port with cheese and biscuits, then coffee. My father smoked one of his favourite Cuban cigars with his coffee.

Not today, he wouldn't, I mused, reflecting on how mores had moved on and how documents such as this gave an insight into social history and evolution. I remembered the furore when the government proposed forbidding smoking in restaurants, then pubs. Now it seemed as distant as 'pea soup' London smogs.

We went upstairs together. I watched the tail-end of the news in my parents' room and also the beginning of a special edition of 'Match of the Day'. For some reason, there were a number of top games being played on the Friday of that week. My father had played American football at Harvard and still follows the sport, but he knows little about soccer, so I had to explain the rules. We saw the highlights of Arsenal against Aston Villa and Manchester United versus Chelsea. That was enough for me. I was feeling sleepy. I'd put in quite a lot of hard work on the river. At dinner, I'd eaten a huge steak — even by my standards. The combination of exercise, a hearty meal, and the alcohol was kicking in. I told my parents I was ready to turn in, we said good night, and I went to my adjoining room, via the intersecting door.

I was asleep within ten or fifteen minutes and slept soundly until about seven the next morning. Because it was a Saturday, I didn't have to be at the river until noon. My parents

*had arranged to have breakfast at nine and I
went to their room at about eight fifty-five.
We went down to breakfast as a family.*

*I did not leave my bedroom between
retiring to bed on the Friday evening and
going with my parents to breakfast the
following morning.*

A page of scribbled, handwritten notes was
stapled to this statement. A detective had
confirmed that there had indeed been a
special Friday edition of 'Match of the Day',
plus the fact that the Arsenal v Aston Villa
and Manchester United v Chelsea games
had been the first two matches screened.
Staff in the restaurant had no difficulty
recalling that the Popes had been the last
diners to leave the restaurant on the Friday
evening. A night porter observed the Popes
ambling up the stairs, locked in animated
conversation. The porter was attracted by the
strong aroma 'from the cigar smoke and
Theodore Pope's sonorous voice. None of
the staff on duty that evening saw Richard
Pope again until around breakfast time on
the Saturday morning.

In the clear, a Detective Ian Samuels had
scrawled at the foot of the sheet of notes.

But he wasn't and isn't, I murmured.
Detective Samuels clearly was no Sherlock

Holmes, but he was probably a retired chief constable by now.

There were a couple of things I wanted to check in Tina Marlowe's statement before I forgot. Had she mentioned smelling alcohol or aftershave on her attacker? Richard Pope had shaved at the hotel before dinner and had drunk a few glasses of wine, plus a port, with his meal. It took me a few minutes to locate the relevant statement and to scan it, stepping-stone fashion over buzz words.

There was nothing in the statement about Tina smelling drink or male perfume. Of course, Pope had been wearing a 'Scream' mask, so his mouth would have been covered, which could have accounted for the absence of smell on his breath. Maybe he didn't use aftershave, though I doubted that. More likely, insufficient questions were put to Tina and Pope. The detectives were just going through the motions, I sensed. They'd written off Pope even before they interviewed him. He was a senator's son, for God's sake. He came from Ivy League stock. He was an Oxford Blue and a big-shot attorney-in-the-making. And so was Ivy League serial killer Ted Bundy.

The more I delved into this case, the more Ted Bundy kept trespassing on my thoughts, like a stealthy pickpocket; just a shadow, but his presence unmistakably there; the nimblest of intruders. Bundy's complete first name was Theodore, the same as Richard Pope's father. Bundy was a sex-thrill murderer. In just two years, he killed more than twenty unsuspecting young women. Like Pope, he was very intelligent, a student of law and psychology. He had even worked in the USA, on a state governor's political campaign committee. In Washington high society, he was talked about as a future president. Political bank-rollers had already highlighted the similarity between Bundy and President Kennedy; both dashingly handsome, both irresistible to the opposite sex, both academic high-flyers.

I even began thinking ahead to the trial of Richard Pope. The defence would argue that he did not fit the profile of serial killers, who were mostly inadequate and dysfunctional, lacking self-esteem, of low intelligence, devoid of humour, friendless and aggressively schizophrenic. Also buried deeply in their subconscious was a compulsion to be caught and recognized. They saw themselves as celebrities, anonymous headline-makers. And it was the anonymity that finally irked them to distraction. They might be filling more column inches than Hollywood stars, prime ministers or presidents and yet, in their mundane workplace and home, they were treated as losers, dross, pathetic nonentities without personality or initiative. The craving for recognition, stardom, induced them to leave little clues. They would be torn by the ambivalence of the need to continue killing for the *sexy* headlines and the urge for exposure so that their co-workers and domineering home-partner would be shellshocked into disbelief and *awe*. They would imagine the reaction: *How could such an insignificant little runt be such a monster?* Monster! Oh, yes, that was such a turn-on word for them. The worse the label, the bigger the gratification. But Bundy defied the rule. So, apparently, did Pope, who was a gregarious young man, confident, talented, successful, gifted with a high IQ, a sporting talisman, fit and healthy, and not a hint of mental abnormality. And that would be the moment when the prosecuting counsel needed Ted Bundy as an antidote, the ace in their hole, the definitive proof that generalizations about criminal stereotyping were flawed. He would be our courtroom match-winner; back from the grave to do a good deed, something he never did while among the living. Good ghosts could come from bad lives.

If there is such a phenomenon as reincarnation, then Ted Bundy could have come back as Richard Pope, I'd already decided, even though I was only a half-day into the case and I'd only Sharkey's word for the DNA clincher.

Theodore Pope's statement said more about himself than anything else. He was fifty-three years old and had been a Democrat senator for ten years. Although he lived in Washington DC, he also owned a ranch in Texas, his home state and where Richard had spent his early years. Richard was their only child and sole heir to the Pope estate, which, all-told, was worth in the region of a billion dollars. As for the Friday evening in question, Theodore merely corroborated his son's account.

I cannot be exact about times, but the three of us were pretty tired when we finally migrated from the restaurant and headed wearily to our rooms. Any big city takes its toll when you're Christmas shopping and I'd spent most of the day trudging around London with my wife, Grace. Richard was also very sleepy. When you're training for the University Boat Race — even in the initial stages — you have to be early to bed and early to rise. He wasn't used to being up and awake after ten p.m. Neither was he accustomed to drinking alcohol, but it was a special occasion — only my second trip ever to the UK and first visit to Oxford, so we had something to celebrate. However, the wine did make Richard very drowsy and he was struggling to stay awake. Very soon after we got upstairs and after watching a bit of soccer, he had to get to bed because he was fighting to keep open his eyes. I also noticed that he was somewhat unsteady on his feet.

Grace Pope's statement was more interesting, particularly the last paragraph.

About half an hour after Richard had gone to his own room, I tapped on the adjoining door because I'd remembered something of such riveting importance I wanted to ask him that I've completely forgotten what it was! Anyhow, there was no reply, so he must have been sleeping. I didn't attempt to go into his room because I didn't want to disturb him. I had no idea whether he had locked the door, though I see no reason why he should have.

So she hadn't tried the door. I flicked through the old paperwork; there was no indication that she'd been asked this question. Did either of them hear any noise from Richard's room, such as snoring, heavy breathing or footsteps? Was there a bandage or a plaster on one of his hands at breakfast? From a superficial examination of the dossier, it didn't appear that these obvious and very pertinent questions had been put to the parents. If they were covering for their son, they would have lied, of course. But at least their lies would have been on record. Neither did it seem that any of the staff on breakfast duty had been quizzed about noticing an injury on Saturday morning to Richard Pope. Already I was beginning to share Sharkey's view of shoddy procedural corner-cutting. Not that it mattered too much now. DNA was a noose that never failed to tighten as soon as the right neck was identified.

After lunch, I returned to the police station, where Sharkey had given me exclusive use of a room that hilariously was called an office. In size, its measurements were somewhere between a solitary-confinement prison cell and a broom closet. But it did have a desk (dilapidated), two chairs (in need of artificial lower limbs), a window (as mucky as a Victorian street urchin's face) and a prototype computer (as slow as motorway gridlock).

The internet had become an invaluable tool for research. I Googled Theodore Pope and quickly came across a comprehensive biography, the most important feature his death three years ago, aged eighty. Grace had joined him eight months later. The gravity of the grave was a fearsome force in uniting separated loved ones. Never mind, the background was useful.

Richard had been engaged twice, once when he was nineteen and then four years later, while at Oxford. *Interesting.* His first fiancée was an Eleanor Reti, daughter of the mayor of Austin. They'd been dating since the age of fifteen, when they'd been students at the same expensive co-ed boarding school. Mayor Reti called the engagement 'a match made in heaven'. Theodore Pope said it would 'unite two important and influential Texas families'. *Spoken like a true cold-blooded, mercenary shit!* Grace believed the couple were 'made for one another' and would 'produce beautiful babies'. *Yuck!* Six months later, it was off. According to Theodore, Richard had come to the conclusion that he was 'too young to make such a lifelong commitment'. Eleanor and Richard had broken off their engagement 'amicably, no hard feelings', and remained 'the best of friends'.

Fiancée number two was a Jackie Reuben, whose father was a state Republican politician. Jackie was three years older than Richard and was an interpreter at the United Nations. She could speak twelve languages, but joked that she had difficulty with American/ English. She met Richard in Washington at a Republican Party ding, but that relationship had cooled and collapsed shortly after he graduated at Oxford. After that, the only mention of Richard was that he had gone into 'government service' — camouflage for every institutionalized sin one could dream of, especially in nightmares.

I started making my own notes.

What were the REAL reasons for the curtailment of the engagements?
Where are those ex-fiancées now?
Did Richard Pope ever marry? If so, is he still married?
Any children to his name — acknowledged or otherwise?
What kind of childhood did he have — emotionally?
Any evidence of abuse in his past — towards him or against others?
How strong was his relationship with his mother?
Was his father overbearing, over-demanding, unbearable?

Back in my hutch, the cheap digital timepiece on my wrist alerted me to the fact that a mid-afternoon drink was overdue. I was fast finding my way around and had already located the two most important features of the building — the men's room and the refreshment robot. Like most police-station vending machines, this one tried to rip me off, promising me change but reneging on the deal. Not until I'd given it a kicking did it cough up. Nothing in this life was ever straightforward. Going nuclear for one's most basic rights had become the norm.

Returning to the file, I again focused on the first case, the murder of Louise Redman. A portrait photograph, presumably from a family album, showed a strikingly attractive redhead. I always flinched at these kinds of happy-family pics in the context of a crime so hideous. Although the colour photo was more than thirty years old, none of Louise's vitality had faded with the passage of time. She seemed so alive, as if trying to speak to me, to tell me something of what happened and who robbed her of the rest of her entitlement. *You owe me,* she was saying. *I was having such fun. I had so many plans. I was going places. I was going to have kids. By now, I'd be a grandma, a success story, if it hadn't been for that bastard who took me by surprise. You now know who it was. Go nail that psycho. Make him pay.*

If there was a way of connecting with the

dead, I wondered how much help that would have been. Very little, I suspected. I doubted that she knew her killer; she'd learn from me. I didn't believe that this was a case in which the victims had been pre-selected. They were simply in the wrong place at the wrong time. If the fourth assault was following a template, then Louise would have been scared witless, as Tina had been, by the 'Scream' mask. But Pope must have spoken. And unless he was a master of speech disguise, she would have instantly tuned into the transatlantic accent. A Yank at Oxford. Not too many of those in that era, especially of his physique. He couldn't afford to let her live; nor the others. Tina was the one that got away and Richard Pope would have been behind bars three decades ago if the detectives on the job had pressed the right buttons.

The only way now to ensure that Richard Pope got his come-uppance was to hunt down Tina Marlowe. There was no DNA evidence to link Pope to the three murders. So the only means of incriminating him for all four crimes was through Tina. The condom ritual was the four-time calling card. Convince jurors that Pope attacked Tina with intent to kill and they would convict him of the murders. The pattern of circumstantial evidence would be crucial — and damning.

But first Tina had to be traced. Then she had to be persuaded to testify. Without her in the witness box, giving a first-hand account, the case was a non-starter. The DNA evidence against Pope, although compelling, would not stand alone for the murder charges. Tina was pivotal. So where would I begin? Only one way: to treat Tina as a missing person. In today's world of data footprints — from tax records to credit card and mobile phone providers — there was no hiding place. Unless you were dead, of course. And that was my one overwhelming fear. A cold case frozen in time for ever.

3

Next day Sharkey was at his desk before 7 a.m. However, cold-case plodding didn't demand Flying Squad tempo: thirty-year-old investigations could be put on hold another couple of hours. On this detail, you danced to the tune of a waltz, not a quickstep. So I'd unilaterally decided to keep civilized office hours: nine-to-five, until the need to rack up the momentum.

Sipping coffee, I went knocking on Sharkey's door.

'Something I can do for you?' he said, the sort of response designed to make you feel a burden.

'A small favour,' I said, straddling the threshold, neither in nor out.

He glanced up, waiting. The size of favours, like everything else, was relative. A request for a thousand-pound loan from a bank was peanuts; from a pauper, it was just nuts.

'I need a partner.'

'I don't run a dating agency.'

How droll! I obliged with a manufactured laugh; just a little one. 'Not *that* kind of partner,' I said, unnecessarily.

'No can do. You're only here because we're so short-staffed. Remember?'

'And I thought it was my talent that had been auctioned.'

Now it was his turn to mimic amusement. 'I can't even spare you a pair of bicycle clips, never mind wheels.'

'There's someone at the Yard I'd like to join me; that's what I'm after,' I said, banter over.

'That's none of my business.'

'I'm hoping you'll make it your business.' I stepped inside his office now, pulling shut the door behind me. 'I'd appreciate your negotiating it with Pomfrey for me.'

'He's *your* boss, not *mine*.'

'But he'll say no to me.'

'How do you know that without giving it a shot?'

'I *know*. But you might have more luck.'

He stretched for his yellow legal pad. 'OK, who is it you want to hold your hand? What's his name?'

'It's a *her*.'

He didn't speak. He didn't need to. His prurient thoughts were telegraphed telepathically.

'Detective Sergeant Sarah Cable,' I said.

'Why her?'

'Because she's good.'

'In bed?'

'As a detective.'

He wrote the name, then tapped the blunt end of his Parker ballpoint on his desk. Looking at me thoughtfully, he said, 'Leave it with me.'

I hesitated at the door. 'I'd be grateful if her secondment was immediate.'

'Leave it with me,' he repeated. 'Anything else?'

'Only that she *is* good in bed, too!'

His face told me that he was a man who responded favourably to self-deprecation.

Back in my stuffy, airless hutch, I returned to the Tina Marlowe documents. She originated from another river-town, not more than fifty miles away, to the east. There was an address in the file and every chance, I reasoned, that at least one of her parents was still alive, perhaps living at the same address. No statements had ever been taken from them (how could they have possibly helped?) but their names had been noted, just for the record, just to tick a box: Ronald and Rosemary Marlowe. There was also a phone number for them.

OK, here we go. Ten rings, then a hesitant, 'Hello.'

'Is that Mrs Marlowe?' I said, trying not to sound like a cold-call telesales pest.

'Yes,' she replied, diffidently.

Voices are notoriously deceptive. Pensioners can sound like bolshy teenagers, while adolescents can come across as comatose oldies.

I rattled through my spiel, introducing myself and explaining that it was essential for me to make contact with her daughter.

I heard what I believed to be a sharp intake of breath, like someone just winded by a blow below the belt.

'Tina's not here. Hasn't been for years. Not since . . . '

I sensed that it would be counter-productive to develop this conversation over the phone. 'These are things that you can explain face-to-face.'

'Oh, dear,' she said, clearly unsettled by my proposition. 'I thought all this was dead and buried long ago.'

This was the trouble with revisiting cold cases, rattling old bones, stumbling on skeletons in cupboards, opening sealed wounds, rekindling memories, some inevitably maudlin, some painful, few comforting.

'When were you thinking of coming?' she added, vaguely, yet seeming to have accepted the inevitable.

'Today,' I said. 'I could be with you early afternoon.'

'My health isn't good,' she said, demurring.

'I won't keep you long,' I promised, disingenuously, having no idea how long the interview might take.

'Well, if you must.'

'See you about three,' I said, underscoring the fait accompli.

'Oh, dear . . . '

That's when I guillotined it, cutting the pipeline of resistance.

★　★　★

Rosemary Marlowe's house was on the fringe of the town centre and no more than half a mile from the sleepy River Ouse that belted Bedford across its midriff, dividing north from south. Mrs Marlowe's home was situated in a leafy avenue on the more affluent and sedate north side, in view of a spacious park, with a bandstand, cricket pitches and a pavilion. The avenue was straight and wide; the Royal Mall in miniature.

As I pressed the doorbell, I saw white net curtains twitch at the edges. When she didn't immediately come to the door, I didn't bother ringing again; I knew I'd been heard and observed. She was taking her time and preparing herself; an ordeal for her, a routine knock-up for me.

'Is that Mr Lorenzo?' she said, croakily, from the other side of the locked and bolted fortress door.

'Detective Inspector Lorenzo, yes.'

A key turned and a bolt was levered sideways gratingly, before the sturdy door inched open, still secured by a security chain.

'Please pass me your ID,' she said; a hard nut for any con artist or burglar to beat.

It must have been a further minute or so until I was considered safe to be admitted.

Mrs Marlowe was diminutive and stooping, leaning on a stick as she led the way, at a shuffle, towards her sitting room. The flower-patterned dress that covered her shapelessly almost reached her fluffy slippers. Even though she wore glasses, it was obvious that she was still severely myopic. The glasses kept slipping and this irritated her as she constantly had to stop to adjust them.

'Where shall I sit?' I said, showing that I respected the fact that she was queen of her castle.

'Take your pick,' she said, indifferently.

The ceiling was high, from which a mini-chandelier, with a cluster of crystal bulb-sockets, was suspended in the middle of the lofty room. There was a white marble fireplace, over which was hung a large mirror, with an ornate, old-gold frame. In the mirror,

I saw the none-too-pleasing sight that had confronted Mrs Marlowe at her front door: a man nearing the threshold of the Big Four-O who had abused himself, but seemed to have escaped, so far, without too many penalty points. But you cannot always judge a vehicle's mileage from its external appearance and rust is easily camouflaged. My coal-black eyes matched my unruly hair. Before we separated, my wife, Patricia, told me that my 'untamed looks' preserved my 'boyish appeal'. But when we parted, she said my features were evidence of a dissolute lifestyle and my *boyish appeal* had transmuted into *immature personality*. My 'fugitive eyes', according to Patricia, were those of a runner from reality, from responsibility and conformity; a Bohemian, but no rhapsody. My lifestyle may have been raffish, but my sartorial judgment had always conformed to Yard protocol. All-night gambling sessions in casinos, too much booze and fast-food addiction had done me no favours, but those vices were behind me — fingers crossed! My weight was coming down. I no longer had to breathe in and hold my breath in order to button my suit-jacket. I could also fasten my collar-button without garrotting myself. Admittedly, there was still some baggage beneath my eyes, but it was being unpacked by the day. Mind you, even when other parts of me had bloated, my face had remained lean, hungry and mean — just like a young Frank Sinatra, before he had ballooned, I'd been told flatteringly. My natural dark complexion made it seem that I was always in need of a shave, even while the aftershave was still smarting. At least six feet tall, I towered over my elderly hostess, who, when bent and buckled, was barely half my height.

I parked myself in a chintzy armchair, fabric fading, beside the fireplace. She placed herself opposite me, lowering herself in aching increments, her fragile, arthritic frame creaking, her joints stubbornly resisting. There were several framed photographs on the mantelpiece, three of them of a beautiful young woman.

'Tina?' I surmised, pointing to the largest of the three portraits that had caught my eye.

She followed the trajectory of my arm with her milky eyes. 'Yes, that's my Tina,' the lump in her throat pulsing her wrinkled neck.

'When she was at Oxford?'

'Just before she went up to Oxford. The same year.'

'Lovely-looking girl,' I said, sincerely.

'Yes. She was very striking, very happy and carefree then. That's how I like to remember her — before the bad times, before everything changed.'

47

'Where is she now?' An opportune moment to go for the jugular.

'*Where is she now?*' she echoed. 'Oh, please, *you* tell *me*. I was afraid you had bad news for me. *More* bad news. Information about . . . well, you know, something dreadful.'

'Nothing like that, I assure you,' I said, leaning towards her, engaging with her intently, harnessing her focus. 'When were you last in contact with her?'

A sea-mist seemed to settle over her eyes. A single tear dampened a pale, pinched cheek, but she made no attempt to wipe it away. 'Years ago.'

I waited for her to elaborate, but nothing came.

'I realize this must be painful for you, Mrs Marlowe, but we believe that we finally know the identity of the man who attacked your daughter — and murdered three young women.'

She reacted without emotion now, as if she'd been drained dry long, long ago. 'What good will *that* do? It won't help Tina. It won't bring back the others, or my Ronnie.'

'*Ronnie?*' I said, puzzled.

'My husband.'

'I'm sorry, but you'll have to explain,' I said.

Mrs Marlowe must have been in her eighties, but seemed to have aged even further since my arrival.

'Tina didn't continue at Oxford; I suppose you know that?'

'No, I didn't,' I admitted; there was nothing about that in the file.

'She came home *that* Christmas and didn't go back. She wouldn't talk to us about what had happened. We thought it advisable not to badger her for details. And the police could disclose only so much. We learned more from the reports in newspapers than from Tina. The police were very helpful. They arranged counselling for Tina, but she didn't stick with it; said it made her feel worse. She also refused to see a psychiatrist. She withdrew into herself . . . completely. Spent days and nights in her room, endlessly. Wouldn't eat with us. Sent out for pizzas. Lost weight, then ballooned. Up, down, up, down, but never upbeat in mood. Always a cloud over her. We tried to focus on the future. You know, about what she intended doing with her life. After all, it had been her ambition, since she was about eleven, to become a politician, a Member of Parliament, and perhaps even make it to prime minister one day. But we never managed a rapport. I so much wanted to connect with her. But all we ever got from

49

her were blank, vacuous looks. Emptiness.'

'It must have been frustrating for all of you.'

She gazed mistily at the portraits, reliving the past thirty years in a few seconds, I suspected, before she said, 'Then she just upped and left.'

'Without warning?' I said.

'Not a hint. Middle of the night. Gone before dawn. Just a note on the kitchen table.'

'What did it say?'

' "Goodbye. Thanks for everything. I know you tried. The fault has been all mine, not yours." '

Tears flowed freely now.

'And you've never seen or heard from her since?'

'I haven't. Ronnie gave up his well-paid job to go looking for her. He was a civil servant in London with the Ministry of Defence. Commuted daily by train. After quitting, he travelled the country searching for her. He even hired someone from one of the country's top private detective agencies.'

'Didn't you report her missing to the police?'

'Oh, yes, straightaway. But because of the note she left, there was nothing to suggest she'd come to any harm or was in danger. She was an adult who'd flown the nest.

Nothing the police could do unless anything untoward came to light.'

'The Salvation Army's very good at finding people who've cut themselves loose from their families,' I said, really posing another question.

'They were one of Ronnie's first ports of call and they were very supportive. In fact, they did better than the PI.'

'They found her?'

'They did, but not until two years after she'd vanished.'

I knew the sequel, but I allowed Mrs Marlowe to tell me.

'They made contact with her, but she didn't want us to know her whereabouts or circumstances. They agreed to act as a conduit, passing messages from us to Tina. We implored her to phone us, so that we could hear her voice, learn directly from her own mouth that she was all right, and find out if there was anything she needed.'

'But the call never came?' I prompted her.

'Never.'

'Was the Salvation Army able to reassure you that she was OK and not at risk?'

'No.' This was uttered with considerable desolation. 'So Ronnie continued his crusade. We'd both benefited financially from inheritances a few years previously, so our finances were pretty sound. We could manage without incomes. I was a teacher, but I was too wrung out to face a classroom of children, happy and bright, just how Tina had been at their age. So I quit, too. Just sat at home, here, brooding. Ronnie was a wreck, taking all sorts of pills; some to help him sleep, others to keep him awake. Anti-depressants seemed to depress him more. Back on the road, he looked all over, but London seemed the obvious place; after all, it is the kingdom of the lost, isn't it? A magnet to runaways.' The question was rhetorical. 'He booked into a cheap hotel around King's Cross and just padded the streets for a full two months, looking hopefully into every female face he came across.'

A wonder he didn't get arrested, I thought, facetiously.

'He was in and out of pubs and clubs. He was becoming increasingly desperate and despairing; I could hear it in his voice. I begged him to come home.'

'But he didn't?' I said, smoothing along the story.

She lowered her head, took a handkerchief from her dress-pocket and dabbed her eyes. 'He started touring escort agencies. I'm sure you know how it works with them. They had photo albums of girls on their books. He was hoping to God to see her face in one of the albums; praying to God he wouldn't. His ambivalence must have stretched him as if fastened to a torture rack.'

I really did feel for her having to relay all this to me, a total stranger. But she was strong. Her fragility was only physical.

'He rang me one afternoon. 'I've seen her!' he said. But there was no real excitement in his voice. What he meant was that he'd seen her photo in an escort agency.'

'Which one?' I said, now poised to make notes, notepad and pen at the ready.

'Something with 'Venus' in the title,' she said, vaguely. 'That's all I can remember. It's such a long time ago.'

'That'll do,' I said. 'I can work from that easily enough.'

'I was bursting at the seams with questions: 'Where is she? Where've you seen her? What's she doing? Is she all right? How have you managed it?' That's when he told me the circumstances.'

'So they hadn't actually met?'

'No. She was on the agency's books as 'Lolita',' she recalled, grimacing. 'The rest of the story is very awkward for me, but you're a man of the world . . . '

'I've been around several blocks a few times,' I said, smiling, trying to make it easier for her.

'Then you'll know all about those agencies?'

'Only too well.'

'The office of the agency was run by a woman. She asked Ronnie if 'Lolita' was the girl he 'wanted'. Obviously, as I wasn't there, I can't recount exactly what was said, but apparently Ronnie indicated that 'Lolita', our Tina, was his selection. He was then asked where he wanted to meet her.'

'What did he say to that?'

'Well, he hadn't given this sort of situation much thought. This was about the fifth escort agency he'd tried, I believe. He was just going through the motions. I don't think he ever really imagined he'd find her along this route. So when he was asked where he hoped to meet her, he was rather stumped. Seeing that he was in a quandary, the woman asked him if he was staying in a hotel. When he said that he was . . . ' Now her voice fragmented and she angled her head away from me, averting her eyes. 'I'm not sure that I can go on with this,' she said, faltering. 'I'm not even sure that I *want* to.'

'Let me help you out,' I said, anxious to prevent her drying up. 'This woman said something to the effect that 'Lolita' would be prepared to go to his hotel room.'

Mrs Marlowe was sobbing quietly now, but

she managed to reply with a nod, before saying, haltingly, 'You can visualize how shocked he was. Apparently he managed to hold himself together and probe a little.'

'Such as?'

'Was she experienced; that sort of thing.' Still she couldn't look at me.

'And what was the woman's answer?'

'That 'Lolita' was one of the agency's most booked girls; that meeting men in their hotel rooms was something she did most days of the week. The full horror of what Tina had apparently become hit him like a sledgehammer to the head.'

'It could have just been sales talk,' I said, as a salve.

'But it wasn't,' she retorted, assertively, having restored her composure. 'A rendezvous was made for 8 p.m. that same evening. The woman wanted to know how long Ronnie wanted to hire 'Lolita' for. Again Ronnie knew nothing about this sort of assignation.'

'So what did he say?'

'Something silly like 'How long is normal?' She told Ronnie it depended on what he had in mind. If he planned to take his escort out to dinner and then return to the hotel, he was looking at a charge for at least six hours; something like a running taximeter. So he said, 'OK, I'll take six hours.' He was very explicit to me later about the actual dialogue. He had to pay in advance; I forget how much it was, but it was a bundle. Another thing the woman said was that if he wanted to pay for *extras*, he'd have to negotiate directly with 'Lolita'. 'What the two of you get up to is none of my business.' After taking the money and as Ronnie was leaving, she said, 'Have fun. I'm confident you'll be back for a second helping after tonight.' Ronnie literally ran from the building and almost vomited in the street.'

'Did he call you, then?'

'No, not until later. He walked and walked, in a trance. Journey's end was approaching. He was on a high, yet he'd also never felt so low. Can you identify with that?'

'I can,' I said, reaching out to her mentally, my thoughts turning to my own daughter. I wondered how I'd cope if I was ever following in Ronnie's footsteps, God forbid!

'I don't know what time he got back to the hotel, but he was in his room for eight, trembling.'

'I take it she turned up? So father and daughter were, in fact, reunited, albeit bizarrely?'

'Tina was a few minutes early. She'd always been a punctilious girl. She knocked confidently. Ronnie threw open the door. And there they both stood, father and daughter, rooted to the spot; her face raddled, wearing the briefest mini-skirt Ronnie had ever seen and teetering on heels more like stilts than stilettos.'

'She must have been stunned,' I said, stating the obvious, just for something to say.

'She was speechless, her mouth cemented in a rictus, bloodless face, Goth-like appearance. Our ghost. 'Tina!' Ronnie exclaimed, thrusting out his arms, moving to embrace her.'

After all those years of searching, he was suddenly within inches of holding her again. The Prodigal Daughter could be taken home. Yet, because of what I'd already been told, I knew the outcome must have been very different.

''No!' she yelled, pulling away from Ronnie and fleeing.'

'Did your husband give chase?'

'Of course, but she was much too quick and nimble for him. She kicked off her high heels and bolted along the corridor, down the stairs, three at a time, out of the front door and into the dusk — and gone. No reunion. Since Tina's disappearance, Ronnie's health had deteriorated drastically, so he was badly out of breath by the time he reached the street. Not a sign of her. A bit like Cinderella, she dropped her footwear — two stilettos instead of a slipper. Ronnie was frantic; distraught. To have come so close and to allow her to slip through his hands — literally! He didn't know what to do. He thought of ringing the agency, but decided that wasn't such a smart idea. That's when he called me to see what I could come up with.'

'And did you have a suggestion?'

'Yes. I said, 'Get on a train; come home.' He said, 'I can't. We were almost touching; close enough to see right into each other's eyes. After all this time, I can't just walk away from it and abandon her.' I wasn't suggesting that he should, but it was obvious to me that he wasn't going to find her again simply by street-walking. He hadn't a clue where to start. She could have been miles away in minutes — by cab, Tube, or any number of buses. Anything he did that night from then on would be futile. My idea was for him to come home so that we could take stock and devise a constructive, cool-headed plan. He needed to take a step back. I was really beginning to think that he should take this new information to the private detective he'd commissioned earlier, but no, he was determined to stick with it; the Lone Ranger.'

She contrived a shallow smile.

'But to no avail, obviously,' I said.

'He stayed at the hotel that night. The

following afternoon, he phoned the escort agency, using a different name from the previous day. He made up a story that a few weeks previously he'd dated a girl on their books, 'Lolita', and he was anxious to date her again because he'd been so satisfied.'

Once again, the outcome was so transparently predictable.

'She said she was very sorry, but 'Lolita' had called that very morning to say she wanted to be removed from the agency's books and her photo be shredded, all of which had been duly done. She tried to 'sell' him another girl, but he hung up; gutted.'

'And finally he came home?' I said.

'No, not right away, not even then. He revisited the escort agency. The same woman as the previous day was running the office and she remembered him, of course. He decided to open his heart to her and come clean.'

'Saying he was 'Lolita's' father and she was his runaway daughter?'

'Exactly.'

A tactic that hadn't a hope in hell — or indeed heaven — of working. Escort agency madams don't do compassion. 'I bet she asked for proof of his story?' I said.

'First thing she said. She was thinking the obvious, no doubt, that Ronnie could be someone with a grudge who wanted to harm

Tina. She claimed not to have an address for our daughter, only a phone number.'

'Plausible,' I said.

'In any case, she said, it was company policy never to give out personal contact details, such as phone numbers, to clients.'

'Definitely true,' I said.

'He got angry and she threatened to call the police. Fortunately, he pulled himself together and then, only then, did he come home. We stayed up all night debating what to do next. We decided that he'd go to our local police station and report what he'd discovered.'

'And what did they say?' As if I didn't know already.

'That she was clearly no longer a missing person. Ronnie had located her. She didn't look ill. There was no reason to believe she'd been harmed. Hard as it was for a parent to take, Tina had made a definite statement that she had no wish to interact with us. She was grown up and we had to respect her wishes, however irrational and unreasonable they seemed. The file would be stamped 'No further action'. Ronnie was dismayed. So deflated.'

I made no comment. Ronnie got the response I'd have given him. The more caring a parent, the meaner the pay-off; that was something else on which I was an empiric expert.

I could sense that the narrative hadn't quite run its full course, so I prepared for the punchline.

'Next morning, Ronnie got up early, didn't bother with his routine shower, dressed, said he was going to buy a newspaper, walked to the railway station, gave the newsstand a miss, and threw himself in front of a train. He went out on an empty stomach. Didn't have breakfast. Not even a cup of tea.'

Mrs Marlowe couldn't see anything hysterical in what she'd just said. That's the way it is when people are traumatized and telling the truth, relating the minutiae of the moment, the mundane madness of it all.

'I had a little item inserted in the Announcements column of the *Daily Telegraph*, recording his death and the funeral arrangements,' she said, bleakly. 'I hoped — prayed — Tina would see it and show up at the cemetery, if not the church.'

More chance if she'd advertised in Time Out, I thought.

'But she didn't show?' I said.

'No, she didn't. No flowers, no letter, no phone call. No Tina. Two departures from my life that I had to reconcile myself with.'

If there was a God, he certainly had a wicked sense of timing, I thought.

4

Sharkey summoned me to his office.

'Shut the door,' he said, not looking up, fiddling with his pen, his jacket hooked over the back of his well-worn, black leather, spin-chair, his paunch a pliable buffer between old, chipped oak and neglected viscera, a light suffusion of sweat shimmering on his florid face. 'I've spoken with Pomfrey.' This wasn't said with reverence; not as if he'd had an audience with the Pope or had made a supplication at an altar.

'Thanks,' I said. I wasn't sure whether to help myself to a chair or to stay on my feet, so I hovered between the desk and the deliberately uncomfortable chair reserved for inconvenient interlopers, so they would always be at an aching disadvantage.

He snorted, pretending to be grumpy, a persona he'd crafted and it suited him. 'Pomfrey wasn't inclined towards your request.'

I guessed that this was a sanitized version. 'I told you he wouldn't be.'

'So you did; that was something you got right. No wonder you're rated so highly at the

Yard.' There was deep-rooted sincerity in his sarcasm and resentment. 'Pomfrey said you're only after a hot-water bottle.'

'That's insulting,' I said, deciding to sit; never afraid to use my initiative.

'My sentiment, too.'

'Anyhow, it's the wrong time of year for hot-water bottles,' I said.

'Bottom line is that your request was granted, albeit begrudgingly.'

I was surprised and it must have showed.

'It's no favour,' he said. 'Pomfrey reckoned Cable would only sulk while you were away and drag her feet; bad for morale.'

'If he really believes that, then he can't know DS Cable,' I said, indignantly.

'Not the way *you* do, apparently!'

I'd stumbled carelessly into that pothole.

'Anyhow, she'll be here this afternoon and she's all yours.' Any innuendo this time was politely concealed. Finally looking up, he said, 'Anything of worth to report?'

'Not of *worth*,' I replied. 'But I interviewed Tina Marlowe's mother yesterday.'

'I didn't even know the old girl was still alive.'

'Tina's father's dead, though . . . committed suicide.'

'Something else I didn't know,' he said, glumly. 'Doesn't seem, though, as if any of this is relevant to tracing Tina.'

'Her mother gave me more leads than she imagined.'

Sharkey raised his overgrown eyebrows. 'Is she in touch with her daughter, then?'

'No.'

'Was she able to tell you if Tina's married?'

'No.'

'Has she any idea where Tina's currently living?'

'Seems not.'

'Does she even know if her daughter's still alive, dammit?'

'No.'

'And this is what you Yard bullshitters call making progress, eh?' He gave me a so-what-the-hell-am-I-missing *now?* gesture, arms raised.

'I said *leads*; nothing definite, but at least now I have a trail to follow.'

'All dead ends have a promising beginning,' he said, negatively; just to be provocative, I surmised. 'Fancy a drink?' he added.

'Too early in the day for me,' I said. 'In any case, I'm trying to kick the juice.'

'That's not what I heard from Pomfrey. Anyhow, I meant a coffee or tea.'

'Too late in the morning for that.'

'*Touchez!*' he said.

The time had come for me to beat a

retreat. From Sharkey's office, I took a 200-yard hike in the sun to Folly Bridge, where I phoned Sarah Cable from my mobile.

'Hi, Mike,' she said, quick to answer her cell-phone, recognizing my number on the screen.

'What time will you be here?'

'About three. Traffic shouldn't be too snarled through town that time of day. Where shall we meet?'

'How about somewhere original, like the Nick?'

'Don't smart-arse me, Mike Lorenzo!'

'Spunky as ever,' I said, blithely.

'No, that's *your* department.'

The template was set for the rest of the assignment.

★　★　★

Sarah Cable, like me, had what's known among fellow cops as a history, the sort of baggage that was always easier for guys to shoulder than the girls, so it was supposed, though I'm not convinced. She'd been locked in a bad marriage with a fellow cop, who was a coward on the streets but always ready for rough stuff in the bedroom. When she filed an official complaint about his behaviour, she was warned about the consequences of 'rocking the boat'. Her immediate superior told her to 'think about it carefully' and not to do anything that would reflect badly on the force. While reflecting, she was treated to a special beating. Next day, after undergoing repairs in the A&E department of her local general hospital, she returned home to find her husband in bed with a woman police sergeant, who was naked except for her uniform-hat, worn at a jaunty angle. Her husband was also naked, except for the handcuffs that fastened him to a bedpost. Sarah booted the woman downstairs and into the small back garden. Still in a rage, she bounded upstairs and threw the woman sergeant's clothes out the window, including the key to unlock the handcuffs.

'Well, well, well,' she said, suddenly icily calm. 'How grateful I am to your *lady* friend! Now I've got you exactly where I've wanted you these past two miserable, sodding years — totally helpless and at my mercy. Oh, boy! I intend to break your head and your balls. Only two questions remain: what with and in which order?'

She chose his riot-stick, which was hanging behind the door. As for the order, she decided to work her way upwards; sort of symbolic.

'You've always been one for clubbing in the West End, now let's see how you enjoy my home-sweet-home version,' she taunted him.

He pleaded with her to be 'reasonable' and not to behave like an asylum seeker; *asylum* as in a place for the insane.

'I'm mad, all right,' she rounded on him, though still composed. 'And now you're going to sample my madness. It looked to me as if you were lapping up being roughed up. Bet I can improve on *her* handiwork, though.'

His subsequent screams alerted neighbours who called the police. Something of a joke, really; a parallel of one of those yarns: *I'm going to send for the police. No need, I AM the police.*

Sarah's husband spent two weeks in hospital and a further three months convalescing, during which time she was suspended from duty. Wisely, he chose not to bring charges for assault and battery, a decision that was greeted with much relief by the image-conscious top brass, but disappointed Sarah. The court case would have been very messy and tailor-made for the front pages of the tabloids. Sarah would gladly have gone to prison in exchange for seeing her husband publicly pilloried. Instead of a sordid trial, followed by gaol, she was privately reprimanded and reinstated, then transferred to the Met from her Home Counties provincial force. And that's how we came to be partners, then pals, and finally something more. Perhaps the reference to *finally* is somewhat premature. The ending has still to be written. Most of the other cops within my orbit were wary of her. 'Watch her, she's bad news; bad as gaol-bait,' was the kind of malicious warning repeatedly whispered in my ear. I took no notice, of course. My marriage had been reduced to flotsam, washed up on a succession of storm-tides. I was drinking too much, gambling too heavily, and bed-hopping like a flea with an itch of its own. Neither Sarah nor I had any right to be judgmental, which was the one thing we had in common. We respected each other's demons and tried to give them a wide berth. Skeletons were best left buried. Dig them up and they could be the most troublesome ghosts, more havoc-wreaking than poltergeists.

My problems were somewhat different in that the past trespassed on the present. Marital separation had not yet morphed into divorce and addictions were as permanent as a birthmark; they could be camouflaged and managed, but they were always lurking on the periphery, just waiting for the opportunity to bounce back. I'll never forget my first attendance at an AA meeting. 'My name is Mike. I'm married. I have teenage kids. I'm a civil servant. (I couldn't possibly admit to being a cop.) I have an ongoing alcohol problem.' *What the hell am I doing here among all these derelicts?* I was thinking, a typical attitude, I was to discover, of newcomers to rehab groups. You don't believe that you belong there. You somehow think that you're very different from the others; that you're a cut above them. Not until that arrogance is stripped away have you any chance of sanitizing your life and finding a way out of the sewer.

Nowadays, I chance the occasional beer, but I don't really trust myself. A pub door opens, boisterous conviviality wafts my way and I'm so damned tempted to go on a bender, pulled inside by an invisible hand. Pub sounds can be as seductive and soliciting as those of an accomplished whore. Getting drunk would be tantamount to breaking marriage vows, which I've done randomly and without remorse, so why be so steadfast now over this commitment? I'll tell you why: to hit the bottle again would be to beat myself up irreparably. I'd be pulling the chain on my career and health. My liver has been punished unfairly, but so far it has stood by me, like a faithful friend. One can abuse that kind of loyalty only so long before it lets you go, casting you adrift, leaving you vulnerable to all manner of predators. When you lose the support of your liver, the gravity of the grave quickly kicks in.

Betting shops had been as enticing to me as pubs; in fact, the two overlapped seamlessly. After a drink, I was emboldened to gamble. If I gambled and won, I was emboldened to drink to celebrate. And if I gambled and lost, I sought solace in alcohol, which merely loosened the leash on any last vestiges of caution. The lure is a soft sell. The steps to hell and ruin are paved with cushions and bordered by roses, the thorns of which have been craftily hidden.

★　★　★

Sarah looked good. Seeing her made me feel better, like a pick-me-up tonic. She was dressed for the street: tight jeans, russet, ankle leather-boots, a loose, white silk blouse knotted at the waist, and her lucky horseshoe amulet around her slender, stem-like neck. You'd never believe from looking at her that she could flatten a heavyweight thug without working up sweat or raising her pulse rate by even one extra beat a minute. Her femininity was genuine, but her delicate appearance was a dangerous trick of nature, designed to trap those who stupidly took her for easy prey. Her sable hair was unrestrained; she chose to allow it to be blown by the wind, like the mane of a galloping horse or a flag fluttering in the breeze. On calm days and when she was indoors, her hair would cover large parts of her dainty features like a hanging, beaded curtain. Most people thought she had a hard, snappy and hostile face; a bird of prey. This was only partially true. She'd survived a very nasty war on the home front. The wounds and scars were inside her head, etched on her psyche. What you saw on the outside was armour, her bullet-proof vest. There were very few people with whom she let down her guard and I considered myself privileged to be the front-runner. Her opalescent eyes could have the look of death about them and then, in an instant, light up a room with sunny mischief. She wasn't a moody person, just introspective; too human, sensitive and incorruptible for the likes of Pomfrey. Too mentally and morally strong, as well. Pomfrey preferred his underlings, especially women, to be pliable and readily manipulated. In that respect, he'd long ago given up on Sarah. And, in other respects, he'd long ago given up on me, until he needed something akin to a miracle. That's when I was known variously as 'The Sorcerer' or 'The Magus', but only when it suited Pomfrey. At other times, his names for me weren't so flattering.

Sarah, as my partner, mostly worked undercover. She came dressed for the street because she'd had no briefing from Pomfrey. All he'd said, apparently, was, 'You'll be teaming up again with that reprobate partner of yours, DI Lorenzo. He's in Oxford, not his usual kind of low-life scene. The only degree he's heard of is the third. He'll give you the story, no doubt doctored, on your arrival.'

★　★　★

'Good to see you,' I said.

She smiled, almost coyly. 'Looks like I could be under-dressed,' she said, noting my suit, even a necktie, though it was loosened, knot resting on my chest instead of throttling me.

'No, you're fine,' I said, 'at least for today. And probably for most of this assignment.'

'Pomfrey said you'd give me the story.'

'Book at bedtime insinuation, huh?'

'No, for once he didn't even hint at that; just said your account would be doctored, no doubt. Snide as ever.'

'You hungry?' I asked.

'Sort of.'

'Let's get a bite,' I suggested, wanting out of my closet.

We walked together, shoulders rubbing like

a couple of tourists, away from the police station, up the hill of St Aldate's. A right turn into the High for a couple of hundred yards, before cutting left through narrow Turl Street, passing Lincoln, Jesus and Exeter colleges, and finally ducking into the compact and intimate News Café in Ship Street.

We ordered tea and cakes, and occupied a corner table-for-two, under a muted TV that was showing silent pictures of a contemporary newscaster, not Charlie Chaplin.

'So, what's the pitch?' she said, finally, putting on her neutral, business voice.

For half an hour she listened and asked intelligent, probing questions, exactly what I anticipated from her.

When I'd finished, she said, as if there had to be more, 'And that's *it*?'

'Sum total,' I said, adding sardonically, 'Nice one, huh?'

'Certainly a new angle — find the victim.'

'I thought it might appeal to you.'

'Do I have a choice?'

'Of course not.'

'Then it does indeed appeal to me!'

The rapport between us was often oxygenated by serrated sparring, not because we were at odds but because it kept our wits sharpened and oiled.

She poured the tea, knowing just how

much milk I liked and the fact that I had sugar only in coffee. Any PI commissioned to do a job on us would have known the score even before the kick-off.

'You believe the mother?' she said, as soon as all the serving was complete.

'Absolutely.'

'No chance that she *does* know her daughter's whereabouts and they're in touch, reciprocating birthday and Christmas cards?'

'Why should she lie — and so elaborately?'

'For Tina's sake. Even for her own sake.'

'Go on,' I encouraged.

'Maybe Tina wants it all behind her. She could be married. Got a family. Her husband and his family may know absolutely nothing about the events here, in Oxford, all those years ago.'

'But she has nothing to be ashamed of — over the attack on her, anyhow. She wasn't raped or sexually assaulted. There's no shame or embarrassment of any kind attached to it.'

'Not in your eyes, Mike, but we're not talking about you. We're not even talking logic or objectivity. You're seeing it purely from a cop's perspective.'

'But of course. That's what we are, Sarah.'

'We can skew things, though. We haven't a clue how muggles see it. For all we know, Mike, it could be the mother who wants the whole thing buried. She'll be coming at it subjectively.'

'Everything you say is possible, even plausible, but I think you're wrong, Sarah. All the old girl's reactions, including emotions, were natural and spontaneous.'

'She's had years to rehearse them,' countered Sarah, always a testing devil's advocate.

'Don't forget, she told me much, much more than she needed to. She could quite easily have left out all the seedy escort agency stuff.'

'True,' she conceded, giving an inch, but no more. 'But by doing so, it's made her tale all the more credible. She could be cuter than you give her credit for.'

'But let's be generous and give her the benefit of the doubt, shall we?' I said, democratically canvassing her vote.

'You're the boss.' Now *that* was a concession. 'Where do we start?'

'No one can simply vanish from the planet these days,' I said, maundering, my mouth lagging well behind my brain.

'But Tina didn't disappear in *these days*.' Sarah was a long way from hoisting the white flag of surrender.

'We're talking thirty years — less from the time she left home — not the Ice Age,' I pointed out, somewhat enervated by now.

'She must have had a bank account, National Health Service and National Insurance numbers and an Inland Revenue file.'

'But no mobile phone,' said Sarah.

I gave that some thought. 'She'll have one now, doubtlessly.'

'If she's still alive. And if she is, she won't be Tina Marlowe, bank on it,' she said.

'And if she's dead, we're wasting our time, because Richard Pope will be well and truly off the hook. At the time of Tina's disappearance, credit cards were in circulation, but not cellphones, so you're right about a mobile trail being a non-starter, unless she has kept her maiden name.'

'And credit cards were nowhere near as rife back then as they are today,' Sarah elaborated on the points she'd been making.

'So let's start plodding, Sarah.'

She waited, like a sniper, for her next target at which to fire.

'Records of marriages and deaths,' I said, in a tone that translated into, *I sincerely hope that this isn't as exciting as it's going to get.*

She considered this proposed starting-point for a moment.

'Beginning with which year?' she said, stoically.

'The year of her father's death,' I suggested.

'Too far back,' Sarah opined.

'Maybe not even far back enough, if your hypothesis is right and her mother's lying. If the escort agency yarn's a fable, Tina could have married soon after leaving Oxford.'

She grinned. 'You got me there, bastard! You want me to hunt the thimble in the marriages and deaths registers?'

'Please. It could be productive, like some coughs. I'll tackle the Inland Rev, banks, and also the escort agency, if it's the one I suspect.'

'Has any escort agency ever lasted that long?'

'There are one or two long-runners. The well-organized ones.'

'And what might *well organized* be a euphemism for?'

'Usually gangster controlled.'

'That's what I thought. And you reckon they'll do Old Bill a favour?'

'More so than a legit outfit, if there is such a thing in that particular meat trade. The last thing they want is heat on their backs, sniffing around, balancing their turnover against their tax returns.'

'So which agency is your money on?'

'Well, Mrs Marlowe believed it had the word Venus in its name.'

'Unless her story was plucked from the fiction shelves.'

'Quite,' I said, my voice transmitting the message that Sarah was labouring her point. 'Venus for the Lonely has been around since the days of the Kray twins and the Richardson brothers. If my memory hasn't started on the slope to senility, thirty years ago the agency was run by an ex-prostitute who'd gone prematurely into whore-management. She was living with one of the 'directors', a Maltese slimeball, related to 'Big Frank' Mifsud. Heard of him?'

'Sort of,' she said, vaguely.

'Mifsud was in partnership with the Jewish East End creep Bernie Silver,' I explained. 'Hard to believe, but Mifsud was a former traffic cop in Malta. Despite being loaded, he dressed like a dosser. They made an unlikely partnership.'

'Why's that?'

'Silver was a north Londoner who'd served in the Parachute Regiment. His vice days began in the East End with a brothel in Brick Lane. That was the beginning of a vice empire that was to bankroll him to the dubious title of 'Godfather of Soho'. Unlike Mifsud, he dressed impeccably and looked like a suave and dapper George Raft in one of those old black and white Hollywood gangster movies. Silver and Mifsud were as disparate as Laurel and Hardy, but not to be taken lightly. Together, they soon owned most of Soho's strip joints. Silver was the brains, Mifsud the muscle.'

'Are Mifsud and Silver still around?'

'No, long gone — the way of the Krays and Richardsons; star-polishers in the great penitentiary of the sky.'

'But what can you possibly hope to garner from this escort agency, Mike? Let's take the mother's account at face value: Tina just quit all those years ago. We're not talking about a company like a bank or the Civil Service or the military that keep personal records indefinitely. The day Tina pulled the plug, everything about her would have been flushed.'

'Wrong.'

Sarah cocked her head like a spaniel, her expression challenging, as if slightly pissed off with me.

'It doesn't work that way, never has.'

'Educate me, then,' she said, her tone unusually churlish.

'Escort agencies and porn-brokers are kindred spirits. They retain everything, pictures, personal details, all the minutiae. Know why?'

'You're supposed to be doing the teaching, but I'll play along: there's always the chance that one of their girls — or ex-girls

— becomes some sort of celebrity, a Mary Poppins-type film star or marries into royalty. Then all the tales of her tarting can be sold to one of the tacky tabloids for a bundle.'

'Or used for blackmail and monthly pay-days for life.'

'Even so, thirty years is a hell of a time to hang on to tat like that. Just think of the number of girls who must have excreted through that agency during that period. Tina's fifty, right?'

'*Right,*' I echoed.

'They wouldn't be expecting her to suddenly become Hollywood's newest discovery.'

'We can mull over this for ever, but we'll never know until we've tested the water,' I sighed.

'So go dip in your big toe,' she said, like she was *my* boss.

'I intend to. Tomorrow.'

'Not too early, though,' she said, impishly now. 'Whore-traders aren't noted for being early birds. They specialize in catching the nocturnal worms.'

Sarah had a flair for anarchy, an attractive feature in a servant of the Establishment.

There was only one important outstanding issue to be resolved that day: where would Sarah stay? The matter was solved early in the evening when I introduced her as my wife to my Oxford landlady, Betty Oliver.

As the two women shook hands, Betty said, 'Been married long?'

'Quite long enough,' Sarah replied, roguishly. She loved these games, especially when I could do nothing but squirm.

5

Venus for the Lonely was situated behind Park Lane, just off Shepherd Market. The premises comprised one room next to a pub and above a bakery. The pavement-level door was locked. Alongside the black-varnished door were three lit-up bell-buttons. The second and third floor bells were for 'models' Melissa and Cristina.

I pressed the button for Venus. A husky female voice said, via the intercom, 'Hell-ooh.' There was heavy emphasis on 'Hell'. The 'ooh' was as in *ooh-la-la*.

'I'm looking for a lady,' I said, confident that the double entendre would be a key to the door, which clicked open, without another word from 'Husky'.

The stairs were the kind I'd mounted a million times in the course of my invasive work in the West End. You could be in one of the most salubrious neighbourhoods, but front doors could be exactly that — just a *front*. And behind those doors could be a moral cesspit. More often than not.

The stairs were uncarpeted. All light was artificial, provided by a single, jaundiced bulb; no lampshade. The peeling walls were painted a sickly green. The first-floor landing creaked under my modest weight. The door to Venus was ajar.

'This way,' Husky called out, hearing my footsteps.

The décor of the office was very different from the approach. For a start, there was a carpet. Alongside a window was a burgundy-coloured chaise longue that was in reasonable condition. Framed soft-porn prints, art deco style, were hanging on all four walls. The rest of the furnishing was minimal. Husky sat behind a large, sturdy redwood desk, on which were stacked black-leather portfolios of the agency's 'talent'; also a couple of white phones and the two-way intercom speaker. I suspected that there was also a red panic-button somewhere down the side of her desk that, when pressed, would bring the blue cavalry to the rescue.

'Hi,' Husky said, cheerily, rising and offering a hand that was decorated with rings on every finger. 'I'm Jasmine, sweet as the flower.'

'Nice,' I said, stupidly.

'And you are?'

'Not so nice. Michael Lorenzo.'

With a fleeting, sickly smile, she said, 'Well, how do you do, Michael? Or do you prefer Mike?'

'I do well, thank you, and Detective Inspector will do just fine.'

For a moment she appeared like a figure in a DVD when you have pressed the 'pause' button. Her large, puffy mouth was stuck half open in a ridiculous rictus, while her darkling eyes were frozen. I held my ID in front of her painted face and sightless gaze, but it was still a few more seconds before the DVD was running again.

'I see,' she said, finally, at last *really* seeing. Her hand was quickly withdrawn before I could squeeze her flesh. These sorts of folk weren't inclined to do handshakes and other welcoming gestures with cops. 'I assume this is a business call?' Her voice had lost much of its husky texture, which must have been fake, like most of her face, though there didn't seem to be much imitation about the breasts that were tippling over the top of her décolletage.

'Strictly business,' I said.

By now she had returned her substantial bum to the leather chair from whence it had risen like a full moon. She crossed her legs, made black and shiny by the tights that submarined down her undulating legs. Her skirt was as tight as a corset, with the hem nearer her navel than her knees. With her long fingers and brightly painted nails, she eyed me suspiciously, in the manner of a wife whose husband has called to say he'll be working late at the office for the fifth successive evening.

'How can I help?' said Jasmine, without much enthusiasm, a touch of cockney creeping into her voice that was now metallic-hard. 'You said you were looking for a *lady*. If that's true, you've come to the right place. We have lots of 'em on our books.' She patted the leather-bound portfolios to under-score her statement, much of her cockiness restored. 'Much of the dating these days is done by Internet. We have our own website. If you visit it, you'll see all the same girls that we have in our albums and you can browse at leisure.'

'I'm not here to make a booking,' I said, inviting myself to sit.

'Then I don't understand. You did say you were looking for a lady, right?'

'Yes, but a specific lady. One who would have been on your books almost thirty years ago.'

The hiatus that followed was filled with suppressed laughter and overt incredulity. When finally she was able to speak, she said, 'There's no demand these days for grand-mas.' She thought she was funny.

'I said the person I need to find was one of

this agency's girls about three decades ago.'

'About the year I was hatched.'

Or spawned. God, she was a scream, so she thought. 'How far back do your records go?'

'When a girl parts company with us, so does her CV.'

She was lying, of course, but it wasn't yet showdown time. Diplomacy always had to be given a chance before going to war.

'How long have you worked here, Jasmine?'

'Five years, thereabouts.'

'Who owns the business?'

Suddenly she wasn't so comfortable, or so jasmine-sweet. Her eyes turned jumpy, as if spooked. 'You want the name of my boss?'

'No, I want the name of the proprietor.'

'Same thing,' she said, petulantly.

'Fine. Give.'

'Do I have to?' she said, weakly.

Now her discomfort was even more pronounced. 'The information you're asking for is confidential. I'm forbidden from releasing those details.'

'With clients, maybe; but not with the police, I can assure you. No, I'll *promise* you.'

'I'll have to make a phone call.'

'It's your office and your phone,' I said.

'Would you mind stepping outside while I make this call?'

'I would mind,' I said, cementing my

position in the chair.

Jasmine scowled effortlessly as she punched a number, going to ridiculous lengths to prevent my seeing the keys she was hitting. Didn't she really realize that, with infinite ease, I could discover every number called, on any day, from this address?

A man answered. 'Yes, *now* what is it?' He spoke so loudly, I could hear clearly what he was saying, despite Jasmine swivelling away from me and pressing the receiver hard against her ear.

'I have a cop here.'

'What sort of cop, for fucksake? A traffic cop? A Keystone Cop?'

Jasmine smirked, suddenly pleased that her boss was shouting. 'Plainclothes. Very *plain-clothes*. Some sort of inspector.'

'Vice?'

'He never said.'

'So what's he want?'

'You.'

'Me! Shit! What for?'

'About one of our ex-girls.'

'Which girl?'

'I don't know. Ask him.'

'Put him on.'

'Here,' she said, sulkily, handing me the phone.

As I introduced myself, oozing civility, I

experienced the disorienting feeling of speaking in a vacuum or echo chamber.

'I hope you haven't got a problem with my agency?' he said, his rancorous tone now dipped in sugary insincerity.

'Not as far as I'm aware,' I said, without menace.

'So what's this about a girl?'

'She won't be a *girl* now. Tina Marlowe, working name Lolita. But that was thirty years ago.'

'Hey, hey, wait a minute, did you say three-zero years ago?' he guffawed, though still cagey.

'I did.'

An exhalation of relief blew down the line. 'Well, that was long before my tenure began. I've had this business less than twenty years.'

'And you are?'

'You want my name?' he said, as if I'd asked for a mortgage loan.

'Just for the record.'

'I don't like being on records,' he vacillated.

'Nevertheless . . . '

'Lenny Diamond. My business is straight, understand? No rackets.'

'Did I suggest otherwise?'

'No, but I just wanted to make it clear. I know you people.'

'*Know* us? Do you mean you're a known item to us?'

'No, I don't,' he protested, trenchantly. 'I'm clean, that's all I meant and nothing more.'

'I believe you. So who did you buy this business from?'

'A guy.'

'A *guy* with a name?'

'Frankie.'

'Just Frankie?'

'Frankie Cullis.'

'And where can I find him now?'

'How should I know? I'm not his keeper.'

'It would help if you did know because then I'd walk right out of *your* life and into *his*.'

Now he had a real incentive to co-operate.

'He moved out of London. Went south, to the coast. Last I heard, he was living in Bournemouth.'

'Retired?'

'Maybe. We never kept in touch. We were never buddies. I didn't even know him that well when I bought him out. I think he opened a bar and started some sort of girlie agency down there, supplying strippers for stag parties and escorts; I heard something like that on the grapevine.'

'In Bournemouth?'

'Bournemouth or Brighton; one or the

other. What's the difference?'

'Only about a hundred miles, three counties, and a culture gap as wide as a strip joint from the Royal Opera House,' I said.

'Not much difference, after all, then.'

'Got a number for him?'

'Haven't you been listening?'

'How about the name of the bar?'

'Inspector, he's been off my radar for light years. Now, that all?'

'For now.' My favourite one-liner sign-off. 'Thanks for your help.'

'Any time,' he said, duplicitously.

I passed the phone back to Jasmine.

With her eyes throwing daggers in my direction, she said into the mouthpiece, 'Sorry to have troubled you again, Lenny.'

'Get rid of the jerk,' I heard Lenny say, snarling.

'Just going,' I said, sufficiently loudly for Lenny to hear.

Jasmine blushed. Bless her. Such innocence! I picked myself up, brushed myself down, and ambled to the door, departing with a one-fingered salute over my shoulder.

'Good riddance!' Jasmine seethed.

'Mutual,' I retorted, resorting to kindergarten retaliation.

6

I lunched on a burger and a double espresso on the South Bank, beside the London Eye. At an outdoor table, in the welcome shade of a tree that smelled as if all the dogs in the neighbourhood had left their calling cards, I phoned the Bournemouth Central Police Station and asked for Detective Sergeant Charlie Mullet. I knew Mullet from his days with the Met. He'd migrated south a few years ago with his wife and two kids, in search of a better quality of life; by that, he meant schools where the curriculum didn't major on designer drugs and how to use knives to achieve maximum penetration. Whether he'd found his Eden, I had no idea. We hadn't spoken since the night of his roistering fare-well shindig, when the rest of us had pooled our pocket money to hire a stripper to mortify him. Mullet was very much a slippers-and-fireside guy, which meant he was probably more suited to the provinces than the big, bad metropolis, where sin was the signature, along with the dog piss.

Mullet was at his desk when he took my call, the first five minutes of which were spent on catch-up. With that out of the way, I said, 'You might be able to help me with a cold case I'm working.'

'With a Bournemouth connection?' he said, perking up, clearly itching for some big-time action.

'Tenuous,' I said, hosing his enthusiasm.

'Oh,' he said, suitably watered down.

'Does the name Frankie Cullis mean anything to you, by any chance?'

He didn't need thinking time. 'You bet.'

My pulse rate increased to a trot. 'I wasn't sure he was on your turf.'

'He's one of our celebrity sewer-rats. A poison-paw in every mouldy pie. What's your interest in him?'

'I'm hoping he's a stepping-stone, leading me to someone else I need to track down.'

'He hasn't made his name down here as a Good Samaritan, especially when it comes to helping the law. He doesn't do favours, unless it's worth his while, which requires a bung.'

'OK, I'm listening,' I said, offhandedly. 'What's he up to?'

'Everything he shouldn't be doing. But he's a skilled tightrope-walker. He somehow manages to keep his footing and, so far, he hasn't fallen into our net. He and his missus run an online dating agency, among other dodgy things.'

'A front for prostitution?' I said.

'Naturally, but they're not brothel-keeping.'

'Living off immoral earnings, though,' I said.

'What other way of living is there for that type? But try proving it. They sail close to the wind, but they're crafty navigators.'

'Have you had personal dealings with them?'

'Several run-ins. Nicked them a few times, but they always walked; spiked by the CPS before I even got them in court. He protests that he's just an Honest Joe matchmaker, trying to broker a little happiness for the lonely.'

'Obviously sainthood awaits,' I said, humouring him. 'What the couples get up to after they're brought together is none of the middleman's business. How many times have I heard that?' My rhetorical question went unanswered.

'Cullis also owns a bar in a sleazy part of town. The Shipwreck. Should be The Flotsam. Caters for tarts, their pimps, drug-pushers, petty thieves and fences. We're always raiding the dump. Make plenty of arrests, but we've never netted Frankie or his beloved, Simone. *Simone*! She's about as French and ugly as the Old Kent Road.'

Mullet's powers of description had improved since he'd become gentrified.

'What's his address, apart from the sewer?'

'Which one do you want? Where he occasionally lives with his wife, such as on Christmas Day? Where he shacks up with his mistresses — note the plural? Or his pond-life bar where he serves watered-down drinks, smuggled wines and spirits, and sells fags that dropped off the back of lorries?'

'Gimme all three,' I said, greedily.

'Best of luck,' he said, after looking up the information for me. 'If you want a guided tour, just give me a bell when you land in town.'

I could tell that he wanted us to get together to reminisce some more, like an old soldiers' reunion, to recall bygone busts in the Smoke, and to regale one another with anecdotes about ex-colleagues known to us both. Met detectives always gassed about quitting the Smoke for pastures new and environmentally friendly, but those who did cut and run never really ever severed the umbilical cord. The pull of the womb was constant, like gravity, and stayed with them until grabbed by the grave.

'I'll bear that in mind,' I said, with no intention of taking up his offer.

'Look forward to it,' he said, equally aware that we wouldn't be speaking again until one of us wanted a professional favour from the other. He had ditched the Met and London, so he was no longer one of the elite. That's the way it worked. There was as much snobbery among cops as in the aristocracy, exemplified by the fact that we Met operators considered ourselves the nation's aristocrats.

Before setting out for Bournemouth, I phoned Sarah to see if she had made progress.

'God, this is mind-numbing!' she groaned.

'Still trawling?'

'Still among the departed, like a warped tombstone tourist. Nothing so far. Just dead ends. Ha! Ha!'

'Nice to see your sense of humour's intact.'

'That wasn't humour, Mike; that was despair. How's your day going?'

I updated her, as succinctly as possible.

'What next?' she said, anticipating my response.

'I go to the seaside.'

'Makes sense,' she said. 'No point return-ing here first, adding unnecessary mileage. Be careful — sounds as if you'll be swimming with the sharks.'

★   ★   ★

I arrived in Bournemouth just before four o'clock in the afternoon. I had some knowledge of this sprawling coastal conurbation, but not detailed, so on the periphery I pulled into a filling station and bought a street-map in the shop. Of the three addresses I'd been given for Cullis, his home was the nearest, so it was logical to try my luck there first.

After a few wrong turns and circling a roundabout three times, I located Frankie Cullis's shack, which was something rather grander than a beach-hut. Its façade was colonial-styled, with a couple of mock Roman columns supporting a portico at the double-door entrance. A black Bentley and a two-door silver Merc were parked on a horseshoe-shaped, pebbled drive at the front of the house, which had been built on rising ground, some fifty yards from the pine-lined avenue. There was a rockery-garden sloping in tiers to a white, pebble-dashed wall of medium height. Although all the houses in this road were of a similar size — in other words gargantuan — the shapes and styles were varied. None of the properties was older than twenty or thirty years, I estimated, though what did I know about such matters? On the opposite side of the road was a golf course, which was also landscaped on a slope. The road must have been bulldozed into a cutting through rising ground on both sides.

No parking was allowed in the road, a by-law I happily ignored. The black wrought-iron gates at the entrance to the driveway of Cullis's property were remote-controlled. However, a few yards from the iron gates was a smaller, unlocked entrance for pedestrians, such as the postman and trades-folk, the route I took.

As I climbed the crooked, stepped path through the rockery, I counted the windows, which were all louvred: four up and the same number down. I reckoned there could be as many as eight bedrooms, two or three bathrooms and probably three large downstairs rooms, excluding the kitchen. Some shack!

The bell chimed. These kinds of houses didn't have anything as common as a ringing bell. I half-expected the door to be flung open by a flunky or at the very least a pinstriped butler. Like most of my expectations, this one was adrift, too. No one could criticize my consistency.

'We don't buy anything on the doorstep, especially insurance,' said the short, balding, portly slob, who showed me nothing below his waist, as he appraised me disdainfully through the sliver of daylight between the doors. Being mistaken for an insurance salesman was almost a compliment. Usually I was instantly taken for a cop.

'Mr Cullis?' I said. He could have been the gardener or handyman, but, in that event, he would have been much more polite and presentable. Especially to an insurance salesman.

'Who wants to know?' He'd obviously had a misspent middle age, watching too many TV soaps.

My ID was already in my hand, which I pushed to within a couple of inches of his unshaven face.

'Shit! Now what?' And before I could answer, he said, 'You're not local, are you?' My ID had been so close to his fugitive eyes that my details must have been out of focus. 'I know all the bleedin' locals. Bane of my life!'

'Met,' I said.

'Then you're trespassing on another force's patch.'

How I loved barrack-room lawyers! 'Do I get invited in or must I mess up your fancy woodwork?'

'What's this about?' he said, holding his ground.

'I'll tell you when I'm inside.'

Reluctantly, he opened the door further and motioned with his head for me to cross the threshold, stand-off over.

'Well?' he said, as soon as the door was shut, not intending to allow me any further than the lobby.

As I repeated my spiel about searching for a woman, he looked bemused, though probably more relieved than anything else, realizing I wasn't there to nick him for an old-bones crime, a legacy of his London days.

'Follow me,' he said, hitching up paint-stained hipster jeans.

As we were about to pass the foot of the stairs, someone above us called out, 'Frankie, what you doing? I'm gasping for that drink I thought you were fetching.'

The voice came from a young woman. Cullis's eyes and mine latched on to the voice trajectory. The woman, semi-naked, was leaning over the upstairs landing-rail, tits dangling.

'Oh, gosh, I'm sorry!' she spluttered on seeing me. 'I didn't realize you had company.'

'Don't matter. It's no one special. Wait in the bedroom,' Cullis ordered. 'This business won't take long.' Then, to me, 'Come on. Let's get this over, so I can get back to unfinished business.'

'Wives can be very demanding,' I said, enjoying the mischievous moment.

'Funny! My wife's in hospital. Broke her leg falling out of bed. Pissed as a priest on Communion wine. Got what she deserved. Legless!' He guffawed at his own pun.

'But are you getting what *you* deserve?' I

said, meaningfully.

'I won't know that until I get myself back upstairs.'

Everything about the house was ostentatious and tawdry, like its owner. The room he led me into was an oversized den, with a pool table at one end and a shiny jukebox in a corner. The walls were adorned with framed *Playboy* centrespreads. A computer sat on a table against the window, a printer on the burgundy carpet. A huge TV screen was pressed against the wall furthest away from the pool table. There was also a cabinet, filled with bottles of liquor, everything from pernod to tequila. The drapes, colour-toned with the carpet, were hung from ceiling to floor, and the leather furniture was all mix but very little match. Someone other than Cullis would have called it eclectic.

As he kicked the door closed irascibly, he said, hands buried in his pockets, 'How long is this going to take? As you've just witnessed, I've someone upstairs whose needs require attending to.'

God, he was funny! He smirked. I didn't.

'It needn't be long,' I said. 'Much will depend on your memory.'

His flabby face creased with curiosity. 'Let's roll, then.'

'When you ran Venus for the Lonely escort

agency, one of the women in your stable was a Tina Marlowe.'

'Who says so?' His hooded eyelids fluttered like the shutters of a rapid-fire camera. His eyes, a road-map of burst capillaries, darted in all directions.

'I say so.'

'What year was that?'

I told him and, on cue, he laughed hoarsely. 'You know how many girls passed through my hands?'

I wasn't sure if his rather repellent defacement of the English language was accidental or an example of his coarse humour. 'Let's just stick with Tina Marlowe,' I said.

'The name means nothing to me,' he said, stubbornly, pouting childishly.

'Her whoring name was 'Lolita'; maybe that will jog your memory.' Now I started to wind him up.

'I've never knowingly employed whores.' For once our eyes engaged.

'We're talking history,' I said.

'Ancient, not modern, by the sounds of it,' he countered smugly, treating me to the sight of teeth as rotten as his life. 'Never a good subject of mine.'

'Look, I'm not here as part of an investigation into any of your activities, Mr

Cullis,' I said, wearily, placing a hand on heart. Pledges, such as swearing on the Bible to tell the truth, didn't carry much weight with inveterate villains like Cullis, so hand on heart was Boy Scout stuff.

'I'm listening,' he said, sceptically.

'I just *have* to find Tina Marlowe.'

'Why, she owe you a blow job?' Regretting his unfettered mouth, he went on hurriedly, 'How do I know you don't want her to testify against me, for something?'

'*Something* such as?'

'Such as something concocted, an invention.'

'Mr Cullis, if that were the case, why would I be searching for just one particular woman, going back all those years?' I said, feigning boredom. 'I'd have hundreds to choose from. Many of them more recent.'

'Whether or not I believe you is immaterial. I don't keep records. Anything that was kept stayed with the agency. You were there this morning, right?'

'I thought this was going to be quick and easy,' I said, side-stepping his smokescreen question. 'Seems like I'm going to have to get a search warrant and return with a posse. And talk with the young woman upstairs. Talk with your wife in hospital.'

For a moment I thought he was going to

spit in my face and throw a punch; perhaps in reverse order. 'You bastards never change, do you?' He unclenched his fist and wiped away spittle from his puffy boxer's lips with the back of a heavily veined hand.

'The decision's all yours,' I said, equably.

'Just what the fuck do you want, exactly?'

'Easy,' I said, placidly. 'The last contact number you had for her. An address. Anything that puts me on to her scent. Perhaps she was friendly with other girls who worked for you.'

'She could be dead. She could have gone to the moon. Ever thought of that?'

'Constantly. Now, are you going to deliver? Get me what I'm after and I'll be gone, like a passing cloud, without the need to rain on your bedroom party.'

'Wait there. And keep your hands off my belongings. No bigger thieves in this world than cops. Especially Met cops.'

He exited the room sulkily, slamming the door behind him, as if using a nutcracker on a sensitive area of my anatomy. I heard him shouting at his frustrated lay. 'Get yourself a fucking drink! I'll be with you as soon as I've got rid of this shite. I knew I shouldn't have gone to the door.'

More than half an hour elapsed before Cullis stomped into the room, sweating as if he'd been to the gym or a workout with the bedroom athlete upstairs, rather than just rummaging through mouldering storage. He was clutching a sheet of paper. 'You're lucky,' he said.

'I'll be the judge of that,' I responded, combatively. With cockroaches like Cullis, it was imperative to retain the initiative at all costs and never to give him any slack.

Squinting, as if myopic, he read from the sepia paper. 'She was shacked-up in Paddington. 59 B, Corsham Gardens.'

'A flat?' I said, reflexly, as I jotted down the address in my police-issue flip-over notepad.

'How the fuck should I know? I wasn't screwing her, if that's what you're fishing for.'

'The grubby thought never crossed my mind,' I said, which was true. 'How about a phone number?'

'Yeah, but what use is that going to be to you thirty years on? Back then it was pigeon-post and jungle drums.'

'Just give . . . please.' The *please* was rather belated, a minimal concession to civility.

'Here, read it for yourself,' he said, holding the sheet of paper to my face, rather than admitting that his eyesight was less than perfect. He probably had glasses, but was too vain to wear them in company.

I knew Corsham Gardens. Only a few weeks earlier I'd made an arrest there, but it was at an even-numbered property. Three decades ago, Corsham Gardens would have been considered a seedy part of town, just a five-minute walk north-west from the railway station. All types of hookers, pimps, drug-dealers and other shady characters had inhabited the ineptly named Corsham Gardens, where there hadn't been a blade of grass, not even in the backyards of the Victorian houses. Litter in the gutters included used condoms. Since then, the area had been given a long-overdue facelift; major cosmetic surgery. It still wasn't even a poor relation of Mayfair, but neither was it home to mayhem. Villains continued to live there, but probably not as many as in snooty Mayfair. White-collar villains; hackers and counterfeiters of designer clothes. Villains who were secretly admired by juries.

'Did she mix with other girls on the agency's books?'

'I don't have that information. The girls didn't mix. I mean, it wasn't a mother's union. Most of 'em didn't know who else was on our books. Why should they have done? It was none of their business. As long as they got work that's all they cared about.'

Made sense, but I didn't concede that. 'What about a photograph?'

105

If looks really could kill, it would have been a good idea for me to keep a finger on my pulse.

'You want blood?'

'No, just a piccie.'

'They've been kept separate from the CV files.'

'So everything *has* been preserved,' I observed, semi-triumphal.

'Not everything. It means another trip to the cellar.'

'I'm obliged,' I said, leaving him no bolthole.

'You look it!' he boiled. The door was slammed so hard this time that the window rattled as if a twister was scything through the area.

Cullis wasn't absent as long as previously. Held in tobacco-stained fingers was a faded black and white pin-up shot of an extremely attractive young woman. He turned it over before handing it to me, as if double-checking the name that had been pencilled on the back. 'You've got everything now, so you can push off,' he said, churlishly.

I smiled again, this time indulgently.

Tina Marlowe was posing provocatively, bending forwards, so that her minuscule bra hardly tethered her substantial breasts, even the nipples were semi-exposed. Her underwear was white and lacy, but her stockings

106

and suspenders were dark, presumably black, though, in mono, one could never be definite about colours. Stilettos streamlined her legs, serving as extensions, a prosthesis, to her lower limbs, making her appear much taller than she really was. Her mouth had also been artificially enlarged by the excessive application of garish lipstick, and the indiscriminate use of mascara gave her panda eyes. The banana held to her lips, Deep Throat-fashion, required no explanation. Her long, glossy black hair, probably a wig, cascaded over her face.

In the photo, Tina was billed unimaginatively as 'Luscious Lolita', plus her measurements, which most likely had a parallel in creative accountancy.

'Is this what potential clients would have seen?' I said.

'I guess,' he answered, indifferently, shrugging; haemorrhaging boredom.

I thought of Tina's father turning over the pages and coming face-to-face with this salacious image of his daughter and trying to reconcile it with the angelic innocence in his deluded mind's eye. His little girl. His princess. Miss Perfect. The daughter with the world at her feet, about to climb life's mountain, up and up into rarefied air. But what goes up must come down. What a fall, even before she'd risen beyond base camp. And hard to explain after what she had been through at the hands of a warped male. But we all had different random recipes for survival, many of them inexplicable and irrational; highlighting the difference between machines and humans.

Mr Marlowe had died long before he'd jumped in front of a train. He must have been dead inside from the moment he saw the daughter he did not recognize; the stranger who had become a lodger inside her body. Body-snatching was as prevalent as it ever was. And the Devil was the fugleman among the snatchers. But this was no occasion for brooding sentimentality or psychoanalysis.

'Who manned the office in those days?'

'Which days?' he stalled.

'I'll rephrase: who manned the office when this woman, Tina Marlowe, was tarting for your company?'

'No one *manned* it. My wife-to-be was what you might loosely call front-of-house.'

'The one who's now in hospital with a broken leg?'

'Yeah, what of it?'

'Nothing. Just thinking, who said the institution of marriage had passed its sell-by date? Perhaps I should have a word with your wife.'

Now he eyed me owlishly. 'Is that some kind of threat?'

'Not at all,' I said, oozing innocence, but I could tell he wasn't the least assuaged. 'I'm assuming she had more day-to-day dealings with the working girls than you did, that's all.'

Anger flared in his shifty eyes at my reference to *working girls*, but he resisted more squabbling.

'She won't remember any more than I do. This is insane.'

'No harm in my trying,' I persisted, mulishly. 'You know how we work. Plod on ticking boxes.'

'Yeah, I know only too well how you *work*,' he said, sourly, giving me a shot of childish pleasure.

Strange how two people could have a conversation and the intimidation by one and the fear of the other were kept under the surface, like the hidden danger of a Titanic iceberg. There was no necessity for me to say, 'And while I'm asking your wife questions about Tina Marlowe, I'm sure I'll be able to slip in a reference to the young woman you've got on hold upstairs.' We read each other's murky minds as easily as computing the headlines of a red-top.

'Which hospital is she in? The Royal Bournemouth or Poole General? I'll take a bunch of flowers with me, say they're from her loving husband.'

'I'd be obliged if you left her out of this,' he said, pleadingly, and suddenly finding some civility.

'Well, that depends . . . '

We eyeballed one another for half a minute or so, in the manner of mongoose versus cobra, before he said, yielding, 'I might be able to give you a lead, after all.'

I refrained from the smugness of a poker player who has bluffed his way to the pot.

'I always made it policy to treat the girls' private lives in the strictest confidence,' he said, as a face-saving preamble before the climbdown. 'I got to hear lots of things, but they stayed *here*.' He tapped his head, alluding to a brain, yet another ludicrous boast. 'Most of the girls, I forget; and that's the truth.'

'But not Tina Marlowe,' I said, finally abandoning sarcasm.

'She called about a year after walking out.'

'Called *you*?'

'Not me personally; the agency. Spoke with Simone.'

'Your wife?'

'She wasn't then; is now. Tina had run out of money. Old story. Didn't fancy office work or serving the pig-ignorant public in a shop.'

'So she wanted you to bail her out?'

'She didn't come begging; that wasn't her style. She wanted to know if she might be considered for special assignments.'

'What's a *special assignment* in your trade? Something like the special of the day at a greasy spoon joint or spicy takeaway?'

'Only the best got special assignments.'

'And how did you define *best?*'

'A combination of brain and beauty. Tina was classy, all right. Very switched on. Really savvy. And as for looks, well, you can see for yourself. She had it all. Special clients would hire a girl for a weekend, or to take on holiday, perhaps on a yacht in the Mediterranean, or just for a one-off important event. Like a couple of times we had girls booked by wannabe Conservative MPs who needed female decoration at their side at candidate selection meetings.'

'Posing as their wives?' I said, incredulously.

'No, just girlfriends, but giving the impression they were an item, with wedding bells possibly soon to be ringing.'

'What did you say to Tina?'

'That I'd bear her in mind. Couldn't promise anything. She gave me a number to call her on.'

'But not the one you've just given me?' I challenged him.

'No, she'd moved,' he said, sheepishly.

'I'm guessing something did turn up for her?'

'About a week later, yeah. A new client. A Russian. An attaché at the Soviet Embassy. The Berlin Wall hadn't yet been bulldozed. East was East and West was West. The big thaw was still some way off.'

'Attaché was the cover name for spy, when it came to the Soviets,' I said, conversationally now, even agreeably.

'I keep out of politics; always have.'

'So what did this attaché want, *specifically?*'

'Good company for a weekend in the country. Intelligent conversationalist. Someone attentive. A good listener.'

'And you thought of Tina?'

'Not immediately.'

'Why think of doing her a favour? She'd quit.'

'She had class. None of our other girls had ever been to university, not even to them redbrick gaffs, let alone Oxford. Blimey! I mean, the others hadn't even changed trains there.'

'So Tina got the *special assignment?*'

'I resurrected her photo and CV, inserting them in my A-list album, and left it to the Russki to make his choice. I didn't lean on him. There was nothing in it for me to push Tina. We'd get our money whichever girl he got the hots for.'

'And he went for Tina?'

'No contest. 'That's the one for me,' he said. It must have been a Thursday because he wanted the booking to run from Friday evening through to Monday morning.'

'A long haul,' I observed, deadpan. Non-judgmental.

'Longer than you think . . . '

Surprisingly, he had me hooked now. 'Go on,' I said, without a clue where this was heading.

'I called Tina, said I might have something for her. She wanted details; usual drill. I told her the punter was a Russki.'

'How did that play with her?'

'No problem. She'd already been with the League of Nations; Arabs to Amazonians. She did ask what his English was like. I told her it was better than most Brits; certainly better than mine, which didn't carry too much weight.' Self-deprecation didn't suit him and he was awkward with it, because it was so forced.

'Of course she wanted briefing on the arrangements,' he went on, smirking unpleasantly.

'Which were?'

'She should come to the office for 6p.m., when Simone would introduce them. 'Pack enough things for the weekend,' I told her. I honestly didn't know at that stage too much about what the Russki had in mind. My policy was not to ask too many questions. The less you know, the less you could be incriminated. 'Course, the girls were always fussing about what they should wear, which was a good attitude, really something I encouraged. It showed they cared about the impression they made, flying the flag of the agency.'

Dropping their knickers instead of hoisting the banner, I thought mischievously. *A new take on patriotism.* He really did believe he'd been at the helm of Britain's call-girl flagship.

'Did she press you further?'

'Naturally . . . about the most important issue of all: the dosh. She whistled when I told her the Russki had agreed to pay her a grand, and that was before any extras she might negotiate with him, which was nothing to do with me.'

'Of course not,' I said, my sneer camouflaged.

'A grand was a helluva bundle of moolah all those years ago. In a weekend, she'd be pocketing a third of the average national annual income. But after her initial reaction, she became suspicious. She began wondering what the punter would expect for such a hefty outlay. She said something like, 'Is he a kinky perv?''

'Were you able to reassure her?'

'Only marginally. I couldn't tell her much more because I was almost as much in the dark as she was.'

'But she went for it?'

'I knew she would. I was in the office when they met. He wasn't my image of a Russki.'

'So what *was* he like?'

'Neat black hair, cut short. Tall and slim, pale-faced. He wore a sober lounge-suit and white shirt with a starched collar.'

'Do you always have such detailed recall of your ancient punters?'

'This one turned out to be very memorable. I guess he was about thirty years old. Good-looking in a conventional, conservative way. Very polite. Very courteous to Tina. She took to him straightaway, especially when he handed over the grand to her in readies, within five minutes of shaking hands. She asked him where they were going and he said he'd rented a cottage in Dorset at Lulworth Cove, apparently a smugglers' paradise in Long John Silver's days. The girls always liked us to know where they were being taken; you know, for security.'

'Was she OK with that?'

'Couldn't wait to get on the road with the loot and punter. I could tell she was confident he was ripe for more milking; cash-register signs flashing in her eyes.'

'Was this punter married?'

'Not then.' For some reason my question had struck a funny-nerve.

'Was he using an official embassy car?'

'Apparently not. He said he'd hired one from Hertz for the weekend.'

'So off they went?'

'As happy as Larry! And on the Monday afternoon she called the agency, wanting to speak with me, urgently. Simone asked if she could take a message, but Tina insisted that it had to be me.'

'Where were you?'

'At home. Simone called me right away and I rang Tina. By then, she was back in London, in her flat.'

'Had something gone wrong over the weekend?'

'That's what I feared. Thought she might have been raped. By a Russki. That's all my agency needed, to be responsible for World War Three! But no. Get this: she wanted me to give her away. The perishing Russki had proposed to her on the Sunday and she'd said yes. Yes! They were getting married. Shocks don't come any bigger. Life's rich tapestry, eh?'

7

Cullis was almost hyperventilating; he was so eager to return upstairs to push on with his pleasures, which had been put on hold. Nevertheless, there were a few more questions that had to be asked, much to his tumescent frustration.

'Did it happen; did they get hitched?'

'Damn right they did — Marylebone Register Office.'

'There's something missing in all this,' I said, puzzled.

'There's something missing for me, too, and it's waiting on ice upstairs,' he protested, his eyes throwing flares.

'Just a few more questions and I'll be gone into the ether,' I promised, struggling to keep this alight, like a candle in the rain. 'Am I supposed to believe that Tina was bowled over in a couple of nights by this Russian?'

'As Tina Turner sang so often, what's love got to do with it?' A ghost of a grin told me that I was expected to acknowledge his smart repartee. I obliged, mimicking a laugh. 'Must have a drink,' he said, shuffling with constipated inertness to a cabinet, where he poured himself a whisky. Declining to offer me one was an elaborate gesture; it wasn't just a matter of deliberate inhospitality, he was anxious not to extend my stay so that he could surrender to the reverse pull of gravity, upwards, without too much further delay.

'So it was a marriage of convenience?'

'Very *convenient*.'

'For whom?'

'Both.'

'Spell it out for me, Mr Cullis, then I *really will* be on my way.' This clumsy dance of diplomacy was becoming increasingly hard to sustain.

'The Russki wanted to defect.'

That didn't surprise me; those were the Cold War days. 'But he didn't need to get married for that, surely,' I said.

'Oh, but he did.'

'Why?'

'Because he wasn't privy to any great state secrets of Soviet plans. Nor was he a scientist or military specialist. He had no info about his country's nuclear programme or military intentions to trade with.'

'He'd have known something about the Soviet's spy network in this country; after all, he was one of them.'

'Worthless info. From what I gathered, our MI5 already knew the identities of most of

118

the spies over here.'

'But perhaps not the double agents,' I said.

'I don't know about that,' he said, pecky as a parrot now. 'But this fella was too far down the ladder to be trusted with really sensitive stuff, I should imagine. The truth was, he'd acquired a taste for our liberal nightlife. Get me?'

'So what was the deal?'

'Tina banked twenty grand.'

'And how much did you pocket?'

'What makes you so sure I got anything?'

'Because you don't strike me as the kind of businessman who'd trade just for sweet fanny.'

'I didn't know nothin' about the plan and the offer until the Monday.'

'But you did give away the *blushing* bride.'

'Fuck you, yes! So what? It was a privilege.'

This was too much, but I didn't want to sever the pipeline, so I chilled.

'Do you remember the groom's name?'

'Not a chance,' he said, petulantly.

'Yet you can recall everything else, including the trivia.'

'We're still talking thirty years ago. Jesus!'

'So, too, was the trivia, yet that's stuck.'

After a sulk, he said, 'His name was typically Russki. Got me tongue-tied at the time. I couldn't pronounce it then, so no surprise it went out of my head yonks ago.'

'Did you keep in touch with Tina?'

'Hardly.'

'I take that as a *yes*, right?'

'She called a couple of times, that's all.'

'Did they set up home together?'

'Not really. Apparently, he rented a place. I believe their names appeared on the electoral roll, just for appearances. But they never lived there together. Certainly not after the first couple of nights.'

'So the marriage *was* consummated?'

'Consummation took place a few weeks *before* the wedding.' This amused him.

'So there was no house-warming party?'

He sidestepped the frivolity. Instead, he answered a question that hadn't been asked.

'Tina left the country with her money.'

'How do you know that?'

'Because she phoned me, to thank me for everything, the night before she flew out.'

'Where to?'

'The New World, the eternal land of opportunity.'

'The States?'

'Isn't that what I just said?'

'Did she say which city she was flying to?'

'LA.'

'To do what?'

'How the fuck should I know?'

'Because I bet you asked her. It would have been the natural thing to do: you know, 'How are you going to survive?''

He downed his whisky with one head-jerk, banged down the glass as if using a gavel on my head, and folded his gorilla arms, resting them on a flabby cushion, his paunch.

'She said something about trying to get into the movies. I didn't take much notice. It was bullshit talk. Sort of thing all airheads say when breezing off to Tinseltown on a whim and a prayer.'

'But she was no *airhead*,' I pointed out.

'You wouldn't have thought so,' he agreed, somewhat churlishly. 'Nevertheless, I took it with a pinch of salt. I just said, 'Oh, yeah. Best of luck, kiddo. Take care of yourself.' She thanked me again and that was it.'

'Was she travelling alone?'

'S'pose. As I said, she'd already ditched the Russki. Neither of them had any more use for the other.'

'Did you ever hear from her again?'

'Nope.'

'You sure about that?'

'Scout's honour! Now, are we done?'

'Almost.'

'Holy Moses!' he fretted.

'You wouldn't know if she travelled under her maiden or married name?'

'No, I don't know, though I'd have thought it highly unlikely that she'd have had time — or the inclination — to get her passport changed from Tina Marlowe.'

'Good point,' I complimented him. 'Enjoy the rest of the day. Plenty of time left to visit your wife . . . I'll let myself out.'

'No, you won't. I want to escort you off my property. I want to watch you disappear into the sunset. I want your footprints rubbed off my land and out of my life.'

'You're a real gent,' I said, my smile as phoney as everything else in that room, especially Cullis.

★ ★ ★

On my drive back to Oxford, I stopped for a fast-food meal at a motorway service station, where I called Sarah. While munching on French fries and a chilli burger, I briefed her synoptically on my day. 'So tomorrow you can abandon the death-trail and concentrate on marriages,' I said. 'Should be a doddle. We have the year and the location of the crime.'

There was a vacuum, diluted only by breathing that amounted scarcely to more than a murmur. Finally she spoke, much to my relief, proving that my staccato account hadn't rocked her to sleep. 'Since when has

122

marriage been a *crime?*'

'When it's a sham. When it's to open a back door to illegal entry.'

Later, in bed, we talked through our respective schedules for the following day. While she was searching records of marriages, I intended making overtures to the spooks at MI5.

'Spooks don't do co-operation,' she said. 'Secrecy is their MO. Even what they have for breakfast is protected by the Official Secrets Act.'

'I have contacts,' I said, optimistically.

'Contacts who were in Intelligence all those years ago?'

'No, but that's why my prospects are good. The info I'm after isn't current. It's something from the archives. Although they wouldn't have been personally involved, they'll have the means at their fingertips to backtrack.'

'Seems to me we're wasting our time in Oxford, then. Although it all started here, it moved on long ago.'

'I agree we are rather misplaced,' I said, sort of helplessly. 'Trouble is, old Pomfrey sees this case as an ideal opportunity to purge his major irritant from his system.'

'And I'm dragged under in the wash of the sinking ship.'

I embraced her, pulling her close, so that our flesh bonded, the coupling sympathetic rather than sexual. Her eyes were melancholy, but not gateways to her soul; their softness was an optical illusion, fortress walls rather than windows. One moment she could be so open, the next moment so closed, but it was this enigmatic chemistry to her personality that made her so piquant. She would never *belong* to anyone again, something that pleased me. Relationships should never be about ownership. No person should ever be someone else's possession. Every partnership should be renewed each day. You should wake and consciously make a decision that the person at your side was the one you wished to continue to call your partner. Conversely, you should be free to make the reverse decision; to walk away unfettered, no one's vassal. Relationships, especially in marriage, could so easily become claustrophobic and suffocating; a union should be a consensus, a unanimous democratic vote. Sarah and I gave each other breathing space. Spending the rest of my life with her hadn't crossed my mind. The next forty-eight hours were far enough ahead for commitment; Sarah's philosophy, too.

Sleep came to us virtually simultaneously, without any further demands from either of us, perhaps underscoring our quirky compatibility.

★　★　★

Next morning, I gave veteran spook Sean Cassidy a call on his mobile. After the mandatory preamble when two people haven't been in touch for a few years, I said, 'I wasn't sure if you were still a paid servant of HM government.'

'Not long to go now,' he said, without enthusiasm and exaggerating his Belfast accent. Sean had been recruited into British Intelligence during the worst of the terrorism in Northern Ireland. He came from the Roman Catholic community of Belfast, but he'd never had any sympathy for the IRA, although his father had been a staunch Republican. Ironically, his father had been killed by a bomb blast and his mother had lost both legs in the same act of terrorism, for which the IRA had boastfully claimed responsibility. For ten years after the explosion that blew away his father and left his mother in a wheelchair for the rest of her life, Sean had worked as a double agent, trusted by the hierarchy of the IRA because of his father's Irish patriotism and anti-British fervour. When the peace deals were being negotiated, Sean was brought in from the cold and had been desk-bound ever since as a handler, naturally specializing in Northern Ireland antiterrorism. Promotion had been his reward for putting his own life on the line, night and day, for so many years, willingly betraying his parents' culture and political religion because of their obtuse bigotry.

'I want some help,' I said.

'You won't get anything that might jeopardize my pension,' he said, immediately on his guard.

'What I'm after is really low-grade stuff.'

'Says you,' he said, sceptically. 'Don't forget, I *know* you of old.'

'I'll explain and then you can decide.'

'Oh, I *will*, rest assured. OK, let's hear it.'

'Are you recording this conversation, Sean?'

'What do you think?'

'You've answered my question,' I said. 'So I'll be circumspect.'

'You mean you'll lie.'

We could have circled the issue endlessly, so I stopped the roundabout.

'I want to talk Cold War days.'

Although he stayed silent, I sensed that the tension was seeping from him in the manner of a slow puncture.

'London, some thirty years ago,' I said.

126

'There was an attaché at the Soviet Embassy who wanted to defect.'

'Didn't they all! Name?'

'That I don't know; that's where I hope you come in.'

'Before my time, dear boy.' Sean was no Irish Mick. His education had been polished at Trinity College, Belfast.

'Of course I know that! Long before my time, too. Your files may be closed, but never shredded. Apparently, this guy was small beer. Not much use to your lot or your sister agency.'

'So we told him to sod off?'

'Something like that. But his overtures would have been documented. After rejection, he hired an escort girl for a weekend jolly and, while fucking her senseless, he proposed to her.'

'Proposed *what*, exactly?' said Sean, the way spooks always played games.

'Betrothal.'

'And she accepted?' he asked, astonished.

'For a price.'

'Good old-fashioned entrepreneurial spirit at work there. I assume you have *her* name?'

'Tina Marlowe.'

'So what *exactly* do you want from me?' he said, seeking clarity.

'Firstly, confirmation.'

'Secondly?'

'The sequel. The Soviets would have caused a ruckus. They'd have wanted their man back — dead or alive.'

'Despite the fact that he was the lowest denomination currency?'

'Pride, old boy,' I said, mimicking Sean. 'Ownership. He *belonged* to them.' Back to relationships — a different sort from those strung together by emotion, but shackling was still a central issue.

'It was probably untangled at diplomatic level,' he reasoned.

'And that's exactly why I've come to you.'

'Let me get this clear in my head: you want the name of the attaché? You want the outcome of the loveless wedding? Anything else?'

'Yes. Where they settled, if at all.' I wasn't going to take Cullis's account as gospel. 'The Russian is only of relative interest to me. I'm seeking Tina Marlowe.'

'Which is unlikely to be her name now.'

'Precisely.'

'Up to a point, this should be a soft pedal for me,' he predicted. 'However, the *point* at which my tracking ends may not take you far enough.'

'But it may drop me at a useful crossroad.'

'True,' he conceded.

'How long will it take you?'

'Depends what's in it for me?'

'How about a kiss on the bum if you deliver within a couple of days?'

'And if I wrap it up for you by tomorrow?'

'Just a big thank you.'

'I'll deliver tomorrow.'

★　★　★

Sarah, working from our laptop, made speedy headway. For several years the national records' office of births, marriages and deaths had gone online. Although she had only Tina's name, that was sufficient. She didn't even need to know the year or location of the marriage, which were bonuses for the search. And there it was before her eyes: Tina Marlowe joined in wedlock with Sergi Cornikov at Marylebone Register Office on 3 July 1979. His age was given as thirty-four; she was twenty-one. A fascinating feature was the groom's address. Apparently, without inhibition, he'd actually used the Soviet Embassy. There was no reason to doubt the Paddington address ascribed to Tina; that appeared to be a neat fit. So we had the Russian's name well in advance of Sean's contribution, but this information didn't assist us one jot in learning anything of the wedding aftermath. Sarah Googled the name Sergi Cornikov, but it didn't produce a single hit.

I haven't the patience for treading water gracefully, but alternatives were limited. We were in the cramped office I'd been allotted in Oxford, where there was just enough room for us to sit next to one another at the desk, staring at the computer-screen, tapping in key words and clicking on 'Search', and bombing out. Like playing Patience and becoming more impatient by the minute.

'Something doesn't quite stack up for me,' Sarah said, idly, filling in space.

'Let's hear it,' I said.

'Tina was a victim of the so-called 'One-A-Month Man'. She was traumatized, naturally.'

'*Naturally*,' I intoned.

'She couldn't articulate her feelings with her parents because she was emotionally frozen, all of which is well-documented, routine reaction to such experiences.'

'So?' I said, somewhat inanely.

'So what strikes me as *unnatural*, to put it mildly, is that she could possibly have turned to whoring. I'd have understood if she'd been turned off men for ever. Or had become a serial killer of men. Wouldn't that be more natural and understandable?'

'Nothing so strange as folk and the human psyche,' I said, perhaps a shade too glibly, because Sarah nailed me with a look that was sharp enough to impale me to the stucco wall behind us. 'Maybe she wanted to make men pay,' I added, giving the subject the serious consideration that it warranted. 'Pay literally. Hit them where it hurts men most; in the pocket. More painful to many than a kick in the balls. Who knows? This is Freudian territory, where we're not qualified to roam. Leave the head-digging and mental excavations to the shrinks. It's not our job to trawl the murky, labyrinthine corridors of the human brain, which too often are more polluted than a sewer. Understanding and interpreting behaviour isn't really our remit; we merely act upon it and that's hard enough. If murder is committed, we catch the killer. It's up to others to make sense of it; more often the *nonsense* of it.'

'That's not entirely true,' she argued, always ready to joust.

'No?' If I sounded huffy, I was.

'No. We have to provide a plausible motive and that demands getting inside heads.'

'Yeah, but with the help of other experts, specialists in that area of expertise. We sub-contract to shrinks, the brain-benders.'

'OK, but don't *you* find it odd that, after

131

all Tina went through and how she froze out her parents, she could so soon drift on to the game and then marry a punter for money?'

'Well, if it was claimed she'd married a punter for love after just one dirty weekend with him, I'd have found that harder to swallow. Look, we're not machines.' I tried not to lecture, but I was. 'You can't calculate in advance how our chemistry is going to interact with other elements.'

'I see what you saying,' she said, thoughtfully. 'Such as with shock.'

'Exactly. A mother can lose her only child in a road accident and the first thing she says is, 'Oh, goodness, I haven't put on the dinner! My husband will be home in half an hour and I won't have a meal ready for him.' Cold as an Arctic winter. And she can remain that way for months.'

'Then it hits her and she crumbles into a nervous breakdown,' said Sarah.

'Delayed shock can play cruel tricks. It's a tripwire, camouflaged, out of sight, waiting to give the vulnerable a fall. There's no template for human nature; no norm. Tina's terrifying ordeal could just as easily have driven her to promiscuity as into the man-hating camp.'

'It still takes some believing, though.'

'The suspension of disbelief is mandatory if you're going to be a successful cop.'

'I thought that applied only to fiction.'

'Fiction has to be plausible. We deal with the implausible. Think about it. The plots to most of the cases that have tested us to the limit have been too improbable for the crime-fiction genre.'

These ruminations dominated the remainder of our day, mainly because there was nothing else to do until we heard from Sean. Even our pillow talk that night was an extension of the topic that had teased our brains for more hours than it deserved.

★   ★   ★

Next day, Sarah and I were just preparing to leave the police station for an early lunch, around noon, when Sean came between us, via my mobile.

'Are you alone?' he enquired, his voice muffled, the way spooks are always so secretive, even if the only information they have to impart is what colour socks they're wearing.

'Yes,' I lied, for the sake of expediency, winking at Sarah.

'OK, well, I've bottomed it out for you. The attaché's name was Sergi Cornikov.'

I didn't tell him that I already had the name. Spooks sulk very easily, especially if

133

they feel upstaged or undermined.

'He'd made several overtures to our agency,' he rattled on, his tone hush-hush, as if he had a hand cupped to his mouth. 'But he didn't have enough to trade with, apparently. He said he could get hold of some really sensitive stuff, but he seemed so desperate that the opinion was that he was too unreliable, an unstable wild card.'

'You mean it was feared that any information he eventually passed on might be made up, just to please you folk?'

'Something like that; pleasers are notoriously bad risks. It was tempting, though, if only as a PR exercise. The publicity could have been used to embarrass the Soviets.'

'Did his people have any idea he'd made an approach?'

'I'll come to that.' Typical of a spook, he wanted me hanging on breathlessly for the punchline, even if there wasn't one.

'After the wedding in London, the couple went to ground. For a few days the Soviets said nothing, then reported Sergi a missing person. A week later, he allegedly phoned his embassy to say that he'd fallen in love with an English girl and had married her. The Soviet ambassador demanded that Sergi be hunted down and returned to them. He accused British Intelligence of having conspired with

134

Sergi, encouraging him to defect. The ambassador said the wedding should be annulled because it was nothing more than a fraudulent stunt and Sergi would be packed off to Moscow, where he would face the consequences for being a traitor, possibly imprisoned for life or even shot.'

'There's no record of this in the media,' I said.

'That's because it was never filtered into the public forum,' Sean explained. 'It was restricted to the diplomatic airways, which became red hot.'

If the pun was intended it didn't resonate in my ear. I had an urge to remind Sean that Tina was my only interest and I wasn't concerned with Sergi's fate, but I was reluctant to offend him, especially as he was doing me a favour that was unlikely ever to be reciprocated.

'How was it settled?'

'I'm coming to that,' he said, reprovingly. 'Because the Soviets apparently were so keen to retrieve their lost property, our boys delighted in taunting their opposite numbers, pointing out that the attaché had legitimately married a British girl on UK soil and he was entitled to stay.'

'Was that the end of the stand-off?'

'Not a bit of it. Sergi was suddenly hot property.'

'Simply because the Soviets were throwing a wobbly?'

'But of course! We weren't interested until they started stamping their feet.'

'Then your predecessors realized he must be a bigger fish than first thought?'

'I reckon it was more bloody-mindedness than anything else. The Soviets' pride had been punctured. Our natural response was to further prick and prod that tender spot.'

'So your lot went after Sergi?'

'The fear was that the KGB would hunt him down first and kill him, to make an example, setting a benchmark, so it was imperative that our side got to him first.'

'I assume the operation was successful?'

'Sergi and Tina were in a boarding house in Weymouth, an old-fashioned seaside town in Dorset.'

'I know where Weymouth is on the map,' I said, indignantly. 'Signed in as Mr and Mrs Smith, no doubt?'

'No, Mr and Mrs Sergeant.'

'Not very smart,' I said. 'It wouldn't have taken the Russians long to have matched Sergi to Sergeant.'

'But we won the race.'

'Three cheers for the Brits!' I said, sardonically. Anyone would have thought Sean was talking about winning Olympic gold. 'Was Sergi taken into protective custody?'

'No, that would have involved your lot, almost certainly resulting in publicity. All police forces are leaky ships when it comes to confidentiality.'

How very true, I thought, sadly.

'He was taken to a safe house.'

'What about Tina, his *beloved* wife?' I said, mockingly.

'She wanted to go her own way, to sod off with her loot.'

'You're intimating that she was restrained.'

'I wasn't around in those days, remember. I'm relying on files, old sepia reports.'

'I appreciate that,' I said sympathetically, doing my utmost to show gratitude and to placate him.

'It appears that she was advised to hang around, just in case the KGB tried to get at Sergi through her. Sergi had told his embassy that he'd married an English girl. They may have unravelled the marriage details in a matter of minutes. If they were already snapping at Sergi's heels, they could have been close to bagging him. There was also the possibility that they might have had Tina in their sights, too.'

'Are you talking *literally* now?'

'No. I mean they might have seized Tina if

she'd broken loose and then they'd have tried to broker a swap for Sergi.'

'So she was moved into the safe house with Sergi to continue cohabitating as husband and wife?'

'For a while, yes.'

Sean ignored my sneering aside. 'Sergi demanded protection.'

'Cheeky bastard! The mess was of his own making. I wouldn't have thought he was in any position to start making demands. After all, you've already stressed he was of no use to you spooks.'

'Top brass decreed we had a moral responsibility.'

I manufactured a contemptuous laugh. 'I fail to see where *morality* came into this.'

'He couldn't be thrown to the wolves. Neither could Tina.'

'The taxpayers might have thought differently,' I said.

'Whatever the rights or wrongs, Sergi was given a new identity.'

'What about Tina?'

'She, too.'

'I trust you have the minutiae for me?'

'Sergi became Paul Barker; very Western. Not a hint of East European in it. He was provided with a council flat in Milton Keynes, a bank account, a job as a hospital porter and a plausible legend.'

He knew that I was *au fait* with spook-speak. *Legend* stood for a fake background and biography.

'Tina was given the pseudonym Juliette Trayner, a single woman whose parents had died in a road accident when she was a child and she'd been brought up by grandparents.'

'What about accommodation for her?'

'A bedsit in Brighton; rent paid for three months in advance.'

'So she'd bagged a bonanza for getting into a bogus marriage and then the state forked out for her pad! What incentive is there for leading a decent life, like mine?'

His chuckle was unforced, I believe. 'If you're decent, I'm a saint. You're a hard man, Mike. Tina had been through a lot. One could argue she deserved a break.'

'Along with thousands of other young women who'd had it tough but had steered clear of the gutter.'

'Pointless being judgmental now,' said Sean, always one for homespun philosophy.

He was right, of course. All that I was now hearing was declaring null and void almost everything related to me by Cullis.

'Was *she* found a job, too?'

'Yep, in marketing, with a hotel chain.'

'Handy for hooking.'

'Give it a rest, Mike,' he protested, still affable, though.

'What about the marriage?'

'Just left on the books.'

'Not annulled?'

'That would only have drawn further unwanted attention to it, requiring explanation to lower echelon bureaucrats and possibly opening up the proverbial can of worms.'

'How long was Sergi mollycoddled by your lot?'

'Not long. As soon as he moved to Milton Keynes, he was more or less on his own.'

'I guess the same applied to Tina?' I queried.

'Even more so.'

'And on that note your files are closed, I assume?'

There was a pause that stretched like elastic having its tensility tested. It was the sort of hiatus that, unlike a vacuum, was bristling with bottled vitality.

'Oh, no, not a bit of it,' he said, eventually, a ripple of *frisson* lacing his voice. 'I don't think we should continue with this on the phone. Where can we meet?'

8

We went for a stroll in the park. Hyde Park.

Spooks have been addicted to talking while walking ever since they saw it on TV and in mid-seventies movies. Reality was soon stalking fiction after authors like John Le Carre had spooks rendezvous on benches in parks, then amble along circuitous paths among dog-walkers and beside lakes, feeding ducks while sharing intrigue and conspiracy that could help to unbalance the world power-structure. Always dressed in bowlers and pinstripes, and armed with a rolled brolly. The caricature became the true character of espionage.

However, the uniform of stockbrokers and City bankers had long ago gone to the charity shops from the spooks' wardrobes. Sean wore jeans, russet-coloured ankle-boots, a matching leather jacket and an open-necked black, silk shirt. To complete his disguise, he even had crumbs for the amphibious birds.

Once again I'd left Sarah in Oxford. Taking her along would have been bad form. Spooks rarely do threesomes, believing religiously in one-to-one special relationships and possessive about contacts. As with a date or an invitation to lunch, you don't take along an uninvited chaperon.

As for my attire, I had on my usual crumpled dark suit, scuffed shoes, a shirt that had once been white, and a yellow tie, which, sartorially, brought a splash of sunshine to the gloom within the rest of my appearance.

'Pleasant day,' said Sean, peering skywards. British spooks regularly relied on banality about the weather as a precursor to cloak-and-dagger skulduggery. 'Any chance of my knowing why you're so interested in the one-time Tina Marlowe?'

'Sure. She was a victim of a very serious crime and could be a witness in a murder trial, if we're lucky,' I said, seeming to surprise him with my frankness, which he probably took for a bogus cover story. These people were not accustomed to trading in truth.

We'd picked up takeaway coffees at the park's café near the Serpentine. I'd paid, of course; a matter of etiquette as he was doing me a favour, which came cheaply at the price of a cappuccino. We drank as we drifted aimlessly and westwards along the towpath.

'This is very embarrassing,' he said, turning away from me.

'What is?'

'The episode you're delving into. You have to give me a promise.' Now he turned to fix me with his penetrating and soulless grey eyes.

'No blank cheques, Sean,' I warned.

He drank some more, giving himself extra thinking time.

'We cannot go on with this unless I have an assurance from you,' he persisted.

'What I've told you is the absolute truth, Sean. My brief is to locate Tina Marlowe, whoever the hell she is today and wherever the hell she is. Nothing else. No hidden agenda. I couldn't care a rat's arse about Intelligence cock-ups.'

Instantly, I knew I'd drilled into a raw nerve.

'Then give me a guarantee you'll never repeat what I'm about to tell you. If I don't have that undertaking we're at an insuperable impasse.'

'You have my word. Satisfied?'

He stopped, took a few steps to the edge of the lake, finished his drink and placed the plastic container on the ground, between his feet, before taking from a jacket-pocket a small cellophane bag, filled with bread-crumbs. In silence, he began sprinkling the crumbs into the murky water. Swans, as elegant as tall ships, glided gracefully towards us, leaving brown ducks, equivalent to bovine, chugging tugs, bobbing in their wake. I knew that it would be counter-productive to rush Sean, so I stood quietly beside him, waiting until he was ready to open up.

'You said something about a cock-up,' he said, eventually.

'I was only speculating,' I said, truthfully. 'Educated guesswork.'

He aimed another handful of crumbs over the flotilla of swans to the straggling ducks.

'Well, you were spot on. About a year after Sergi Cornikov was set up in Milton Keynes, one of our officers happened to be dining in the restaurant of a West End hotel.'

'And he ran into Sergi?' I speculated.

'Wrong. He saw Tina. She was dining with someone he recognized immediately. A government minister.'

'Who?' I said, perhaps a shade too eagerly, my interest overtly salacious.

'On a need-to-know rule of thumb you don't need to know,' he said, peremptorily.

'Spoil sport!' I said, hoping to lighten him up, failing, of course. 'Did Tina recognize the Intelligence officer?'

'No, she'd never met him. He'd been involved only behind the scenes in her case. Our man wasn't working. He was with his wife. It was their wedding anniversary, but he couldn't take his eyes off the politician and his dinner-date.'

'That must have gone down like salmonella with his wife.'

Still no smile.

'They were very animated together. Both very tactile. They knocked back two bottles of wine. Large brandies with coffee. In his report, the off-duty officer described Tina as looking like a 'princess'.'

'Not like a tart?'

'Top whores are as clever at concealment as top-flight Intelligence officers.'

'And there speaks a man who's in the know!'

A wisp of a self-congratulatory smile flickered momentarily, like a candle in the wind. This was a mountain-climb for me.

'Was any of their conversation overheard?' I added, genially.

'Apparently not. The officer upset his wife by insisting they stay in the restaurant until Tina and her escort shifted.'

'Then they followed, like a Mr and Mrs Clouseau?' I said, immediately regretting my flippancy.

Sean grimaced. 'Tina and the minister didn't leave the hotel. Instead, they headed for the lifts.'

'So she was back to her old *tricks*,' I said, the double entendre wasted on Sean.

'Our conscientious off-duty man made a call.'

'To base?'

'That's one way of putting it. His rank

entitled him to pull someone out of bed.'

'Not Tina or the errant minister, though,' I said, once more misusing my mouth.

'Our man at the hotel waited to be relieved.'

A very rude retort popped into my head, but I managed to keep that one suppressed. I'd already gambled enough with my irreverence.

'Not the best of ways to round off a wedding anniversary evening,' I observed, visualizing the scene: stiff upper-lipped spook in dinner-suit, wife in evening gown, the pair skulking behind a mock-marble column in the atrium, under glittering chandeliers. Very spoof James Bond.

'His wife lost her rag and left him to it.'

'Bravo!' I said. 'Women's lib rattled yet another musty male cage.'

Sean still wasn't amused. 'Do you want this story or don't you?' he said, petulantly.

'Sorry,' I apologized.

'Yes, well, a surveillance op was mounted.'

'On Tina or the minister?'

'Both.'

'So two were pulled out of their sacks?'

'Male and female. The man was assigned to Tina, who exited the hotel at around 4 a.m., taking a cab to an address in Church Street, Kensington.'

'Classy neighbourhood. What about the politician?'

'He left the hotel about half an hour later.'

'Obviously had trouble getting his socks back on.'

Sean's groan was all in his eyes and expression. 'He went by taxi to his flat in Westminster.'

'Which wasn't his family home?'

'His main home was in his constituency.'

'And where was that?'

'How naïve do you think I am? Identifying his constituency would be tantamount to naming him.'

'Not even a good try, was it?' I ridiculed myself.

'Agreed. However, let's stick with Tina because that's your brief, right?'

'Right.'

'She was renting in Church Street.'

'Expensive.'

'Yes, very, even for a basement flat.'

'What about her Brighton pad?'

'She'd given that up within a few weeks of being housed there; her job, too. Inquiries were made discreetly in Brighton.'

'Some gratitude for all the state's generosity!'

'It gets better.'

'Don't you mean *worse?*' I said.

'The more intriguing it becomes, the *better* it is for us. On the afternoon following her tryst with the minister, Tina went to another hotel in the West End for a rendezvous of some significance. Can you guess with whom?'

Frivolity again led me astray. 'The US president? Mickey Mouse? The Pope?'

'Have you always been such a pain?'

'Ever since I was born. Nothing more painful than childbirth. Ask any mother.'

He sighed exasperatingly. 'Waiting for Tina at the hotel was our dear old friend Sergi.'

'A husband-and-wife reunion,' I said, trying to remain inscrutable, though with mentally raised eyebrows.

'While talking in the lounge, they also had afternoon tea.'

'Very British,' I said. 'A real salad-days scenario. How long were they together?'

'More than an hour. Then they stood, shook hands again, and she departed. He hung about for five minutes or so before also leaving.'

'Where to?'

'We had only one man at the hotel. He followed Tina to her Kensington flat. The whole case had to be reopened and reassessed. At a case conference, it was decreed that there should be round-the-clock surveillance on Tina *and* Sergi, and that the government minister should be watched as much as possible, though that wouldn't be so easy.'

'Was the surveillance to incorporate electronic eavesdropping?'

'What do you think?'

'I'm asking.'

'There was bugging, yes. Don't forget our deal on this; nothing goes beyond this moment.'

'Everything you're telling me is ring-fenced. It stays here.'

Poor old Sean was still as cautious as a tightrope-walker without a safety net. 'It was essential we bottomed out as quickly as possible what was going on. Three days after Tina's tea-time meeting with Sergi, she took a call from a man who introduced himself as a friend of a government minister, whom he named. He said that she came highly recommended and wondered whether she would dine with him.'

'And she said?'

'She'd be delighted to, but obviously needed to know who he was.'

'And who *was* he?'

'Again I'm not divulging.'

'OK, but did *he* tell *her*?'

'He said to call him John and hoped she'd

be content with that, for the time being.'

'Did your people identify the caller from his voice?'

'Oh, yes, there was no doubt about that. There's much more, though, to this than you might be imagining. They arranged a date for that evening in the Ritz. She asked him if she should go 'prepared for a late night'.'

'I just love those euphemisms,' I said. 'Top-drawer whores have a way of sanitizing everything. They're alchemists, trying to gold-plate everything about their tatty lives. What was his answer?'

'He said that, in his job, he was accustomed to all-night sessions, to which she replied, 'I understand. I'll come prepared. Are there any special requirements?''

'And were there?'

'He said that anything of that nature could be negotiated over dinner, rather than on the phone.'

'Rather late for circumspection,' I commented.

'Even more significant is what followed. As soon as that call was over, Tina phoned Sergi, giving him chapter and verse, seeking instructions.'

'So Sergi was handling her?'

'Totally.'

'For blackmail?'

'Not conventional blackmail. It became transparent that Sergi had never really been serious about wanting to defect. In essence, he was still working for the Soviets. Their protests about his marrying an English girl and settling in the UK were pure theatre. He was acting under orders, a puppet of the KGB.'

This didn't take much computing and I was instantly ready with my next volley of questions.

'Was he still slumming it in Milton Keynes?'

'Very much so.'

'And his place and phone were bugged?'

Sean simply nodded, almost indiscernibly. 'Soon after Tina had agreed to the dinner-date at the Ritz, she called Sergi, outlining her itinerary — and, importantly, asking him for suggestions re the way she should play it. She'd become a *sister*, that much was indisputable.'

Again he fell back on the international jargon of spooks: a *sister* was a female agent whose job was to seduce and sleep with *targets*.

'What directions did he give?'

'He said not to press him on anything, that she should allow him to make all the running and allow the conversation to take its natural

151

course. He knew the minister would immediately become suspicious and guarded if a whore began asking questions about, say, nuclear physics.'

'Just a little bit!' I laughed. 'Even if the whore had been to Oxbridge.'

'Sergi's guidance to her was instructive for us. He said, 'Just compromise him; that's all we need. Do that and we have him on a leash for life.' He told her to do anything possible to entice him to her flat. Not to fuck at the hotel, which wouldn't have been wired.'

'Did she succeed?'

'Without much effort. Around midnight, after several bottles of wine, including champagne, enticement was unnecessary and hidden cameras captured them fucking. Tina's flat had been secretly entered and searched at some stage. No damage caused. Everything left as found. She'd never have realized there had been a forced entry. The peeping-tom cameras were located; state-of-the-art gear; professional equipment. Unless Tina was an electronics wizard, she'd never have been able to install such sophisticated hardware. Neither could she have operated it by herself.'

'What happened to the compromising pics?'

'The first part of my answer is conjecture:

they were probably filed away in the Soviet Embassy, with the idea of using them for political — not financial — blackmail. The prime minister was tipped off. Two politicians were confronted and demoted. Returned to the backbenches.'

'Making them worthless currency for political blackmail,' I said, demonstrating that I had paid full attention.

'The pics did surface, however. They were given gratis to a Sunday scandal-sheet, as a means of discrediting not just the two MPs but also the government; depicting Western decadence, etc. The MPs didn't stand for re-election at the next General Election, so the Soviet spy network had achieved a limited return on its investment.'

'Was Tina a known radical?'

'No. Her philosophy was that of the capitalist; a free marketeer. The Soviets were putting business her way. You could say that they were *her* agents, finding her work, for which she was paid twice.'

'By the Soviets and her sleeping partners,' I said, perversely impressed.

'A nice little earner,' Sean agreed, almost admiringly. 'She was in it purely for the money. The Soviets were masters of honey-traps. Tina was perfect for their range of black arts. The last thing they wanted was

153

someone with a left-wing extremist political agenda because someone like that is driven by ideology and is one-dimensional and might as well be wearing a badge of allegiance. She needed to be intelligent, attractive, mercenary, self-disciplined, a free-thinker, flexible, manageable, ruthless and amoral, but most definitely not an overt tart. With Tina, all the boxes were ticked.'

'Was any action taken by our side?'

Sean gave this question more consideration than any of my previous ones.

'It all ended very abruptly,' he said, cagily.

'Is that a *yes* to my question?'

Sean avoided eye contact. 'Sergi was discovered dead in his home, an empty bottle of pills on his bedside table. An empty bottle of scotch on the floor.'

'He'd overdosed?'

'Well, that's what the coroner said.'

'Is that what *you're* saying?'

He just shrugged.

'No suicide note?'

'Of course not.'

'So it *wasn't* suicide?'

'Don't think so.'

'Accidental?'

'Hardly. The pathologist had a problem. The OD was massive: barbiturates, which are an old-fashioned drug, rarely prescribed

154

nowadays; not too much in those days, either. The margin between a safe and a fatal dose too narrow. Oddly, there was no residue in his stomach.'

'So how did he explain the mystery?'

'Only one explanation: the fatal dose was injected straight into the bloodstream.'

'So if self-administered, there must have been a used needle nearby.'

'But there wasn't.' Now he eyeballed me as an evil, bitter-sweet smile trickled slyly across his enigmatic face.

'So the OD couldn't be matched to the empty drugs-bottle?'

'Correct.'

'How about the booze? Any evidence of alcoholic poisoning?'

'He would have passed a breathalyzer test.'

'As mysterious as Marilyn Monroe's death, eh?' I suggested.

'But without the headlines. There wasn't one reporter at the inquest. The press didn't follow it up, even when the coroner recorded an open verdict.'

'Sergi was murdered?' I concluded, in the form of yet another question.

'That's one possibility.'

'What are the others?'

'None that immediately spring to mind.'

'And who could possibly have wanted him

dead, other than your lot?'

'His paymasters, the Soviets. But who cares? You don't, do you? You've stressed constantly that your involvement is motivated only by Tina.'

'You got me there!' I conceded. 'So what happened to Tina? She must have stayed on the Intelligence radar.'

'Only briefly.'

'Go on, then, finish the story,' I urged.

'She was scared shitless when she heard about Sergi's fate. Within two days she'd sold her car, drawn out a large amount of cash from her bank account, packed her bags, and boarded a flight to the USA.'

'Where was her point of entry?'

'LA.'

At least that was one fact Frankie Cullis got right.

'What reason did she give for entering the US?' I said. 'I assume that she didn't tell US Immigration that she was on the run.'

'Vacation. Immigration, as was normal procedure then, allowed her a stay of up to six months. Rubber stamped.'

'Were the CIA tipped off?'

'Eventually. And the FBI.'

'Can you define *eventually?*'

'Matter of weeks.'

'Is that it?'

'Yep.'

'No follow-up?'

'Nope. The file went to the vaults and gathered dust and the hue of jaundice, only to surface in the last few hours — for your benefit.'

'No requests for further background from the CIA or FBI?'

'Not that's in the file.'

'She simply disappeared into the ether, is that what you're saying?'

'Doubtlessly reinventing herself. Survivors always do. They develop feral instincts and antennae. They become chameleons, morphing into whatever it pays them to be.'

'If she stayed in the USA, it would have been as an illegal immigrant,' I surmised.

'You don't know that, Mike. She might have married a rich Yank. Sergi was dead, so she was free to re-marry without a divorce. Till death us do part: she'd won early release. She may have become legitimately employed and given a green card, for all we know. There have always been lawyers in the States willing to bribe bureaucrats to issue Green-Card work permits for their foreign clients. By now, if still alive, Tina may well be a naturalized US citizen. Voting for the Republicans. A diehard Tea Party stalwart. A Stars and Stripes patriot, lamenting the dissipation of moral standards and Christian virtues in decadent Western society.'

'You think? Sounds to me as if her mantra's more likely to be, *Screw the lot of 'em!*' I said, cynically.

'She'd already achieved that!' observed Sean, his humour finally breaking through.

9

'It seems to me that I'm superfluous to requirements,' said Sarah, obviously inviting a contradiction. 'You might as well return me to sender. 'Can do very well without, thank you.''

I suspected that she was seeking reassurance that her input was a constructive contribution and that she wasn't a passenger, kept on board purely for company and night-time entertainment.

'We're a team, a fifty-fifty partnership,' I said, sincerely. 'It's impossible to forecast who will get the breaks.'

'So far they've all come your way,' she said, not jealously, just concerned about being much more than a sleeping partner. The one thing you could always say about Sarah was that she continuously pulled way above her weight.

'The important thing is that we both keep pitching. When the game's over, we'll have broken even, you see.'

She thanked me with a reserved smile, not completely assuaged. But she was genuinely pleased with the progress made, albeit ponderously. Rather than an action thriller, this was a sedate drawing-room drama, characterized by subtle manoeuvring and delicate finessing, advancement by minimal increments and not with one gigantic leap. We now had new names which Tina Marlowe might have been using — Tina Chekov or Juliette Trayner — and a location, LA. Of course, she could have re-married, giving her yet another different surname. But there would be records in the USA; also bank, credit card and phone trails. The next step was across the Atlantic.

Firstly, though, Sharkey had to be brought up to date.

'What's the strength of your information?' he asked, sceptically, with his first question.

'Gold-plated.'

'Can't you be more specific?'

'No.'

'Why not?'

'Because I was sworn to secrecy. Without giving that guarantee, I wouldn't have made this breakthrough.'

'You call this a *breakthrough*?' he taunted me.

'Well, it's certainly a breakthrough along-side the previous thirty years of inertness on behalf of my predecessors working this case in *your* force.'

Sharkey grinned boyishly. He enjoyed a playground scrap.

'So you're angling for a freebie holiday in Tinsel Town, playing with Hollywood cops?'

'Without going to LA we'll be at yet another impasse,' I said, in a take-it-or-leave-it tone.

'Not sure if I can swing it,' he said, in the pressured manner of a manager faced with a request for a pay rise. 'What with all the cutbacks and economy drives. How do I sell it to my chief?'

'As a *fait accompli*,' I suggested.

'I'll see what I can do,' he said, snorting, his way of dismissing me from his office. 'You may have given your *gold-plated* contact a guarantee of *omerta*, but you're not getting any promises out of me.'

'Well, you can only do your best,' I said, getting up and leaving languidly. Just before the door closed behind me, I poked my head through the gap, adding, 'Oh, I almost forgot, I'll need two airline tickets. One for me and the other for my partner, Detective Sergeant Sarah Cable.'

Then I bolted.

★ ★ ★

Forty-eight hours later, I was boarding, with Sarah, a United Airlines flight from London Heathrow to Los Angeles. By then, Sarah's uncertainties and misgivings were ancient history.

Before leaving Oxford, I'd made contact with the LA bureau of the FBI and the Los Angeles Police Department, advising them of our travel plans and smoothing the way for assistance; routine international police protocol. We would have no jurisdiction outside the UK, so there could conceivably be situations that required US cops to act as our agents, therefore building a trusting relationship from the outset was paramount.

Reservations — two separate rooms, of course — had been made for us at a Holiday Inn in Santa Monica, just a couple of hundred yards from the Pacific Ocean, the period-piece pier, the glorious beach and the palm-lined promenade, where chess players and skateboarders co-existed harmoniously.

After the twelve-hour, brain-numbing flight and crashing through so many time zones, we were in no mental or physical state to focus on our assignment, so we ordered an early meal from Room Service and were asleep before putting out the cart in the corridor for collection.

When we awoke, it was morning of the next day, with the sun already high in a vibrant-blue sky, with only a handful of wispy clouds, like loitering jetstreams that had been cut up and rolled into floating party-balloons.

★ ★ ★

Following breakfast and several coffees around the pool, I spoke on the phone with a Lieutenant Dan O'Malley of the LAPD. He was friendly enough, but it was readily evident that he wouldn't be breaking sweat or burning rubber on our behalf. Finding a witness to a batch of thirty-year-old murders in Britain was no big deal in the land where serial killers were endemic and notched up tallies resembling phone numbers. Single-number killings were small beer.

O'Malley beefed about ridiculous work-loads and staff shortages. Forget his accent and it could have been any administrative cop in the UK griping.

'I'd love to help,' he said, 'but . . . '

There had to be a *but*, the preface to every cop-out; an appropriate pun in the circum-stances.

'We're not going to get far over here as Lone Rangers, not without badges that carry a punch,' I said, sort of plaintively, though trying not to sound too wimpish.

'The best I can do is put you in touch with

a PI,' said O'Malley. 'But don't think I'm fobbing you off.'

That's exactly what I was thinking.

'Charley Emerson is a one-woman, spectacular show. She's talented, honest and her rates are competitive. She won't rip you off. Neither will she give you the runaround with bullshit. If she isn't getting anywhere, she'll come clean and won't attempt to keep the meter running. If you like, I'll call her first. She owes me a couple of favours. Maybe I can persuade her to forego a charge until she's done some groundwork and has an idea about the possible outcome. She relies heavily on our co-operation, so it's in her interest to keep our relationship nicely oiled.'

Clearly this was going to be the best — and only — offer on the table.

'I'd be obliged,' I said, garnishing my voice with sincerity. 'What can you tell me about her, apart from the fact that she's competent and doesn't cheat her clients?'

In an instant, he was into auto-pilot. 'Ex-cop. Divorced, naturally. Husband's still with the LAPD. One kid, in her custody. Mother cares for the boy while Charley's working a surveillance. Been in business a couple of years. Works from home. Contact number is her cell-phone so clients and the opposition don't have her address, though anyone determined to get to her could soon find out where she rests her head. She's in a dangerous game for a lone female, but it's her choice. Must be turned on by the roll of the dice, I reckon.'

'I know the type,' I said, eyes on Sarah, who cocked her head curiously.

'She has long black hair; well, she did have when I last saw her, which was a couple of months ago. Green eyes. Toned figure. Jogs two miles daily ahead of breakfast, before the heat rises. A smile that can melt a Mafioso's heart. When she seeks a favour, she rarely has to pay for it. If you don't lust for her, your testosterone-reservoir must have dried up.'

I was glad that Sarah was standing away from the phone so that she couldn't hear O'Malley, who hadn't finished his monologue.

'She's sassy and feisty, alternating from one to the other, a trick that she doesn't even know she's performing. Mother's Irish and father, who died a year ago, was Italian. A fiery mix, huh? I need say no more.'

I knew he would, though.

'She never goes out without a gun in her handbag and another strapped to a shin, under her pants.'

For someone overworked in an understaffed department, O'Malley was certainly being generous with his precious time.

'How old's her kid?' I asked.

'About ten.'

That gave me a handle on Charley's age.

'As I said, I'll have her call you,' he continued. 'Then the two of you can work out together how to play it.'

'How soon?' I pressed.

'As soon as we're done, I'll start the ball rolling.'

'We're done,' I said, thanking him before guillotining the connection.

★　★　★

Charley Emerson came to us. We arranged to meet poolside at 4.30 that afternoon.

She was exactly as described by O'Malley, although her eyes hid behind reflector shades. Her hair was allowed complete freedom, some of it falling over her face, apparently without irritating her. Her jeans were sufficiently flared to allow for a weapon to be attached to a lower leg without being outlined. A white, sleeveless silk blouse hung loose over her thighs. Prominent cheekbones and a modest mouth sculpted her face into a magnet that turned heads. She wasn't as tall as I'd visualized, but her sheepskin boots gave her lift. O'Malley was right about her having

166

style. Her poise and posture were all-Hollywood as she sashayed towards us. Picking us out was easy for her because there were only a handful of people at the white, plastic tables around the rectangular pool and a couple of teenagers skylarking in the water.

I had a chair already pulled out for Charley, whose smile was indeed *melting* as she reached us. Politely, she removed her glasses while we shook hands with her, giving us a close-up of those green-for-danger, Irish eyes, inherited from her mother.

She said yes to a drink: a double espresso, no sugar. Sarah and I had already drunk in one day more than our ration of caffeine for a week, so we both ordered iced orange juice from the waitress who patrolled the pool area solicitously.

'How much did O'Malley tell you?' I said.

'Next to nothing,' said Charley, her voice much softer than I anticipated.

'Not surprising, because he knew next to nothing,' said Sarah.

Charley treated us both to that killer smile of hers; a Great White masquerading as a skittish dolphin, I suspected.

'OK, so what is the storyline?' said Charley, true to the soundtrack of Hollywood.

In order to avoid any possibility of compromising her loyalty, I left out the name of the male identified as the 'The One-A-Month Man' and the fact that he was a CIA agent. Charley made notes, jotting down the names Tina Marlowe, Tina Chekov and Juliette Trayner. I also refrained from mentioning anything about Tina's whoring and becoming mixed up in the murky world of espionage. Although I had forewarned law-enforcement agencies of our itinerary, I'd kept the purpose of our visit very narrow: the pursuit of a witness to a cold-case series of murders; no less and certainly no more. Never muddy the waters if it can be avoided.

'The beginning should be easy, a mere formality, establishing her entry into the country,' she said, tapping her notepad with a silver Cross pen. 'After that, who knows . . . I'll just go where it takes me.'

'I ought to make something clear upfront,' I said, my discomfiture difficult to disguise.

'Let me say it for you,' said Charley, once again taking off her shades to treat me to another dance of those tantalizing eyes. 'You're saddled with a tight budget?'

'Wrong. We *don't have* a budget.'

Now Charley's eyes lost some of their luminescence.

'Let me clarify, we're not hoping to free-load,' I started to explain.

Some of the radiance returned.

'We thought we'd be getting action-assistance from the LAPD.'

'But sweetheart O'Malley has off loaded you on to me.'

'In a word, yes,' I said.

'And you require fiscal approval from your brass in the UK?'

'Spot on,' said Sarah.

'After my talk with O'Malley this morning, I didn't expect him to move so fast,' I said.

'He didn't,' said Charley. 'I'm the fast-mover.' Any shadow that had been cast over her had been washed away. 'I presume O'Malley put you in the picture about me; that I'm an ex-cop?'

'He did,' I said, simply. 'His summary of you amounted to a star-studded testimony.'

Charley was as susceptible as anyone to blarney, another of her Irish heritages.

'So I know how these things work, how bureaucracy can be the biggest obstacle,' she said. 'But if they've sent you this far, I can't see them allowing a few hundred bucks to come between you and a result.'

'That's sound logic, which isn't something our hierarchy is renowned for,' said Sarah.

Charley toyed with her empty coffee cup as she said, 'I owe O'Malley.'

I didn't let on that O'Malley had mentioned that to me; to have done so might have been to break a confidence.

'Normally I'd demand a retainer and an advance on expenses, but I'm prepared to forego those formalities for a couple of days, by which time I should have some idea how much work is going to be involved.'

'And we should have clearance from our chiefs,' I said.

'Well, I don't think we can take this any further today,' said Charley, standing and proffering a hand, very direct and business-like, to which I warmed. 'I live quite a way from here, in the Valley, and I have a young son to collect en route. This time of day traffic will be gridlocked on the freeways. I'll make a start for you in the morning and I'll be in touch as soon as I have something to report.'

'Good to do business with you,' I said.

'Likewise.'

We had lift-off.

10

Part of the deal with
should call him once a
report.

On the morning after o__ ....ccung with
Charley, I could tell Sharkey no more than we
were still 'bedding in' — not a very clever
choice of words, but he resisted reacting
coarsely, much to his credit and unfamiliar
restraint.

'Don't forget, you're not on holiday,' he
once more reminded me, as a footnote.

I decided not yet to mention Charley to
Sharkey. Tactically, it made sense to leave her
out of the equation until I was able to 'sell'
her as an indispensable asset and ally.

It was a further forty-eight hours before we
heard again from Charley. Sarah took the call
on the bedside telephone of her room, just as
we were about to head for breakfast. After
exchanging a few mundane pleasantries, she
passed the phone to me.

'OK, I'm making headway,' said Charley,
going straight to the viscera. 'The subject
entered the USA as Tina Chekov. She rented
a duplex in the Valley, not far from where I

of fact. Blue-collar neighbour-
was in LA less than a month.'
did she move to?' I enquired, eagerly.
as. She got a job in a casino. Front of
se.'

'Without a work permit?'

'No, it was legal. She'd been issued with a
Green Card.'

'How did she swing that?' I asked,
fascinated. 'I'd have thought it necessary for
her employer to prove that the job couldn't
be done by an American?'

'You're missing a crucial factor: in those
days, the Vegas casinos were Mafia-controlled.
They had all kinds of government officials on
their payroll, not just cops, politicians, judges
and mayors. For them to get someone a Green
Card was as easy as buying a hot dog.'

'But why should they have gone to that
trouble for Tina? She was a looker, undoubtedly, but there's nothing exceptional about
that in LA or Vegas, surely?'

'Not many with a cute English accent,
though; a precious commodity in certain jobs
over here. Something a lot of people, me
included, are envious of.'

'Where did you get all this info about
Tina?'

'Sources. You know the drill, you should
know better than to ask me that.'

'Of course. Sorry.'

'Pardon granted. However, there's more.'

'You have me salivating.'

'Spare me such details, please! The casino was the Sandstorm. On The Strip, but only just. Not one of the biggies. However, it was Mob-owned and there was a big push to improve its Strip cred. Heavy investment was underway. The Mob was using its muscle to get celebrities like Sinatra, Dean Martin and Sammy Davis Jnr to show up, not necessarily to sing, but just to mingle and be photographed purporting to be playing the tables. Punters were flown from here, LA, San Diego and San Francisco, with their air fares paid for them. Accommodation rates at the Sandstorm were drastically pruned. Booze was free and plentiful; anything to entice the high-rollers. Once at the tables and plied with alcohol, the casino's outlay would be recouped tenfold. This is all documented history. Vegas folklore. The important handle for you to hang on to is the inherent corruption within the state of Nevada, where the Mafia was king, not Presley, during the relevant era. Elvis merely sang for the king. So putting Tina on the payroll, securing her a Green Card, making her legit, was a kind of daily transaction, something left for a Mob minion to deal with.'

173

'Is Tina still in Vegas?' I said, hoping not to sound impatient.

'No, but I'll come to that. Let's stick with chronology.'

'You're the storyteller,' I said, amiably.

Meanwhile, Sarah had drifted to the balcony, where, to the west, she had a view of the ocean and the beach, under a cloudless canopy. To the east, however, downtown LA and the Valley were almost totally obscured by a shroud of sulphur-bloated, low-hovering smog. Somewhere in that lung-congesting pollution was Charley, on the end of a phone-line, talking with me; in another climate. Might as well be on another planet. Life in LA could be deadly dangerous, long before taking a bullet.

'I've been talking with a guy who was a dealer at the Sandstorm.'

'A drugs dealer?' I cut in.

'No, no, a dealer at the tables; blackjack and a roulette croupier.'

'Got you!' I said, feeling a shade foolish.

'He left Vegas when the Sandstorm closed. Later, it was bull-dozed and is now a medical clinic. He's retired and lives alone in LA in a rented, two-room rat-hole, but he remembers Tina Chekov.'

Now I became wary. Vegas casinos were awash with women: gaming addicts, croupiers,

174

waitresses, hostesses, showgirls, man-hunters and hookers. Why should he recall one of them, someone very low in the pecking order, from all those years ago? Despite O'Malley's endorsement, I began to wonder if Charley was spinning me an elaborate yarn just for the commission; taking me for not just an out-of-town sucker, but an out-of-country sucker.

'Why should he remember her?' I challenged Charley, though not overtly aggressive.

'Because she didn't stay front of house for very long. Because she made a name for herself. In addition to making a nuisance of herself.'

'Pray tell how did you make a name for yourself at a Las Vegas casino, unless you were Elvis or one of the Rat Pack?'

'Simple. She became the favourite of the boss, the chief exec.'

'You mean she became his mistress?'

'And in doing so made an enemy of the woman she deposed. Apparently, the catfights were legendary. Front-row seats could have been sold for big bucks. One night a couple of blackjack tables were overturned, spilling all the chips and cards, and the two women had to be pulled apart by a couple of Security heavies. Tina eventually became known as the 'Duchess' because of the way she lorded it around the joint, flicking fingers at waitresses

175

and getting people fired if she took a dislike to them.'

'Did the boss have a wife?'

'A long-suffering one, but trying to divorce a mobster is tantamount to breaking the Mafia law of *omerta*; you're likely to lose a lot more than an arm and a leg.'

'So tell me how it all ended in tears in Vegas for Tina?' I said, echoing my guess, which I estimated was an educated one.

'One night, as she climbed out of her white convertible in the casino's parking lot, someone stepped from the shadows and flooded her face with acid.'

Momentarily, I was speechless. I was transported in a mental time-machine to Mrs Marlowe's home in Bedford, where I was looking at the portrait of that truly beautiful young woman, Tina. A face that since then had been deliberately scorched with acid. I remembered everything that Mrs Marlowe had said about her daughter and everything was skewed. But that was life, I'd learned. Every sinner had once been a saint in a mother's eye.

'What was the outcome?' I said, with a sinking feeling, fearing that Tina had gone to the worms and maggots years ago.

'She was rushed to hospital, naturally. Doctors saved her life.'

Relief!

'They didn't save her face, though; nor all her sight.'

Renewed consternation. If we did trace Tina, would she be up to testifying against 'The One-A-Month Man'?

'So she was partially blinded?' My question was a cocktail of panic and hope, in just about equal measures.

'She lost all sight from one eye.'

'Permanently?'

'Permanently, yes.' Cold-bloodedly and even heartlessly, she added, 'Quite a price to pay for fucking around with people.'

'Did they catch the assailant?'

'No. It could have been a man or woman. There were no witnesses. The attacker didn't speak. Tina screamed, but no one was seen running from the crime scene. The boss's ex-bedroom playmate and wife were questioned, but their alibis were bullet-proof. Someone was probably paid to do it, which is the way it works around here. Standard MO.'

'Was there no money trail? Someone would have been paid. Not the sort of thing someone would do just for love.'

'Maybe not for love, but most certainly for hate or lust.'

'*Lust?*' I said, baffled.

'Yes, you know, a promise of action

between the sheets could have been a sufficient temptation. If the truth be known, the cops were probably not too fussed.'

'Why's that?' I asked, for no other reason than professional curiosity.

'Because of what she was. Because the Mob didn't like bad publicity. And any story that frightened away punters was the worst possible publicity. It hit the place it hurt most — their pockets. Tina was in hospital for weeks, her face swathed in bandages. She received flowers daily, but in all that time not one visitor.'

'Did that info also come from your dealer contact?'

'No, I've spoken with a Nevada sheriff. He pulled the file for me. I promised him a Christmas card.'

I smiled knowingly. The world was turned by the same axle and grease wherever you stood or worked.

'When she was eventually discharged, Tina called the boss man at the Sandstorm. He agreed to meet her at a diner off the Strip for a coffee and doughnut. On the phone she'd said she wanted to talk about returning to work. Of course, he'd long ago engaged a new sleeping partner. Apparently, when he saw Tina's face, he told her she was fired and barred her from ever setting foot again in his casino. He walked out, leaving his drink and doughnut untouched — and the tab for her to settle.'

'A real charmer,' I said, 'but how would the police have known about that conversation?' I needed to forensically test the veracity of everything I was being told in order to form a view about Charley's credibility.

'They didn't. I got this from the retired dealer. Apparently, the casino boss strutted around the joint, boasting about how he'd booted off the payroll the world's ugliest whore, whose only chance of making a living was in a freak show.'

I had a suspicion that the story was winding down. 'OK, so what became of her?'

'Well, there was nothing left for her in Vegas and that's the end of the first chapter, which comes free. Anything else, you're going to have to pay for.'

'So you don't know where she went?'

'Not yet.'

'The problem is, as I see it, Tina could have flown literally anywhere,' I said, downcast. 'And how long ago was that? At least twenty years.'

'A big hole to fill, I admit,' she said. 'But not as deep as it was twenty-four hours ago and when you left the UK.'

'Spoken like my kind of philosopher,' I said, agreeably.

'Call you same time tomorrow. Ciao.'
'I'll be here,' I said, into a vacuum.

★ ★ ★

I postponed breakfast for a few more minutes while I phoned Sharkey to update him, deciding that the time was now ripe for introducing Charley to him vicariously. By then, Sarah was squatting beside me on the bed, a hand on my shoulder.

'You've done what!' thundered Sharkey.

'Only way we were going to get anywhere,' I said, equably.

'You have no authority.'

'Used my initiative,' I said provocatively, winking sideways at Sarah. I could have taken a blood-pressure reading over the phone.

'What about our special relationship with US law enforcement?'

'Doesn't come on the cheap any more. They're too busy fighting their own crime. Now let me give you the good news.'

As I brought him up to date, so all symptoms of astronomically high blood pressure receded.

'And what's our national debt come to so far?'

'Zero,' I said, giving time for this to sink in.

'Nothing!' he enthused, as ecstatic as a man facing bankruptcy whose debt had been wiped out by a mysterious benefactor.

'A goodwill gesture,' I said.

'From a PI? I don't believe it! Are you bullshitting me again or have you found a fairy godmother among thieves?'

'No bullshit and she's no fairy.' Without histrionics, I sketched for him the arrangement with Charley.

'Well, as long as you dig up Tina, alive and serviceable, I suppose we'll be able to get it through our tight-arsed accountants,' he said, grudgingly. Then, with a rare flourish of kinship, he added, 'Not like it used to be, when there was a bottomless pit to fund speculative fishing trips. Now it's like running a pawnbroker's shop, always trying to undervalue everything and getting things on the cheap.'

Hyperbole, of course; nevertheless, it captured the mood of most of us who were supposed to sanitize the streets with a decimated workforce — sweepers with fewer and fewer brooms.

★ ★ ★

'So he bought it?' said Sarah, as I hung up.

'Sharkey isn't buying anything. He hasn't the beans to buy. We're the peanut cops.'

'But we continue?'

181

'For now. He can't afford to keep us here indefinitely. Neither can he afford for us to give up the chase. Like the world economy, he's in a black hole. However, if Charley comes up with the goods, we'll ensure he honours *that* liability.'

'And in the meantime?'

'We hit the restaurant for a mega breakfast and make a further dip in Sharkey's black hole.'

'If we're going under, we might as well go down like the *Titanic*, in style, band playing.'

A kindred spirit, indeed.

11

For the next two days we were able to continue swanning around as if on holiday, despite Sharkey's little lecture. We lounged around the pool, sunbathed on the beach, ate late breakfasts and lunches, and dined alfresco at leisure. We were rudderless until Charley returned to give us a steer.

When we last spoke, Charley promised to phone 'same time' next morning, and she didn't let me down, but it was only to say, 'I've put out lots of feelers; still waiting for call-backs. Talk with you tomorrow,' which she did, bang on cue, but only to repeat, almost verbatim, the previous message.

And then:

'Have you two had breakfast yet?'

'No, Charley, but we're just about to.'

'If you can hold fire for another forty-five, I'll join you at the banquet.'

'Will it be worth our suffering hunger pangs?' I answered, convivially.

'Yes, oh, yes . . . on my life!'

'Then we'll happily starve,' I said, speaking for Sarah as well as myself.

'I'm already on my way to my car.'

Sarah's face and eyes were ablaze with questions, which I addressed as we headed for the lifts.

★　★　★

We waited in the lobby, sharing sections of the *Los Angeles Times*. Charley came through the entrance as if propelled by a hurricane, hair flowing like that of a galloping thoroughbred. Her cop's eyes vacuumed the scene in one sweep and she made us without breaking stride.

'Hi,' she greeted us, as I tucked the newspaper under my arm.

'Let's eat,' I said, dispensing with formalities.

Charley was dressed similarly to our first memorable encounter, though now she carried a suede briefcase, which suited her better than the weapon in her shoulder-handbag and snub-nosed miniature that caressed her calf.

'Lead the way,' said Charley, which I did.

A waitress poured us coffees. The food, hot and cold, was at the buffet counter. Charley snapped open her briefcase, which she'd rested on her legs. I was famished for food, but even hungrier for information.

'Business before we eat or after?' said

184

Charley, removing papers from her briefcase.

'Before,' I said, overruling my grumbling stomach, which gave me an acidic-kicking for being so inconsiderate.

'OK, what I've been doing is exploiting my contacts in the IRS and other similar agencies, plus banks, credit card companies, and cell-phone network providers. Only people living rough on the streets can ever avoid the radar of national bureaucracy, Big Brother, the ultimate voyeur. The most important news for you two is that Tina is alive.'

'Where?' I said, on the edge of my seat now, unable to restrain myself.

'Still in this country. She became a US citizen some ten years ago. She pays her taxes. She has no sheet. She has two bank accounts, three credit cards, and a Black-berry. Oh, and she's a pillar of society, with one child, a daughter. Although not married, she's in a longstanding, stable relationship. After fleeing Vegas, she underwent cosmetic surgery here.'

'In Santa Monica?' I enquired, for clarification.

'Don't know . . . and that's the truth. Suffice it to say, it was somewhere in LA.'

'Was it a complete reconstruction job?' Sarah asked, always one for the minutia.

'Apparently.'

'Very expensive,' intoned Sarah, half-question, half-statement.

'Maybe not as much as you think. The surgeon is the father of Tina's child.'

Stick my face back together again and you can fuck me to the moon. Not an unreasonable assessment of mine, I reckoned.

'So Tina's in LA?' I said, arguably upbeat.

'No, she's in New York City. Queens district.'

'Living with her creative knifeman, the designer surgeon?' I surmised, as if stating the obvious.

'Oh, no; that was an affair that lasted under a year. He was already married and remains so; well, that's my limited understanding.'

Another twist in the maze. Where were we heading now?

'What's she doing in New York?' Sarah asked.

'She runs a refuge for women victims of domestic violence. Any abuse, really.'

'Very laudable,' Sarah commented, without spin or undertow.

'So when did she find God?' I wondered aloud, argumentatively.

'Good Samaritans may be rooted in biblical legend, but since when has a religious belief been mandatory for humanitarianism?'

said Charley, her question both abrasive and rhetorical.

I raised my serviette as a white flag of surrender. 'What's her partner do for his daily bread?'

'*She's* a management risk assessor,' said Charley, without blinking.

I turned to Sarah. She turned to me. Eyes locked, before we both eyeballed Charley, who was enjoying the moment, playing us like an angler with two stunned fish on one teasing hook.

'You mean her lover's a woman?' I said, trying not to sound incredulous, but failing.

'It's not exactly a phenomenon,' Charley replied, searchingly. 'Why should you be surprised?'

I had to think about that because it was an iceberg question, with hidden implications and the ability to sink reputations and credibility. 'Because of what she was doing in Vegas. Because of what she'd been doing in London. Because of her having a child.'

'Proclivities change, you know,' said Charley, turning me into a Stone Age relic.

I held up my serviette yet again.

'Now to a much more sensitive matter,' said Charley, roguishly and fidgeting, head bowed as if in prayer. She crossed her legs, left over right; then right over left. She twiddled a pen, rearranged her paperwork, and pitched a sightless gaze somewhere over my head.

'Tina's partner is a Laura Farrow. A little younger than Tina, but not much. She's away from home a lot — on business.'

'Assessing risks for companies, I assume?' I interjected with what seemed to me a logical assumption.

'That's what Tina believes.'

'You mean Laura's two-timing on Tina?' said Sarah, female angst festering.

'Not the way you're imagining. Laura isn't a management risk assessor; that's just a cover, but, for it to be foolproof, not even her closest family must be privy to the truth.'

'Then what the hell is she?' I said, wanting an end to this suspense.

'She's with the CIA, but you don't know that, OK?'

★ ★ ★

By mid-afternoon, following breakfast with Charley, we were aboard a United Airlines flight to New York.

By the time I called Sharkey from my cell-phone at 36,000 feet, an hour after take-off, it was gone midnight in the UK. I had Sharkey's home number and my call woke him up.

188

'Hello,' he growled, gravelly, in a tone that translated into: *Who the fuck is this? Have you no idea what the time is?*

'It's Lorenzo,' I said, a tad too cheerfully for someone just ear-bashed from their sleep.

'What's up?' he said, startled, reasoning that a call at this hour could only be from a harbinger of woeful tidings.

'We have an address,' I said, starkly.

There was silence as his brain, still sleeping, struggled to compute such a skeletal statement.

'What the fuck are you blathering about?' he demanded, steaming; his voice rattling like a kettle on the boil. 'I know you have an address: you're at the Holiday Inn, Santa Monica. Are you on the juice again?'

'We have an address for Tina,' I said, spacing out the words, as if talking to an idiot or someone who barely understood English. 'She's in New York. We're on a flight there right now. With luck, we'll connect with her first thing tomorrow, local time.'

'Christ!' Suddenly he was wide awake, fuelled by an adrenaline rush. 'Is this straight up?' he added, a stupid question prompted by the need for reassurance that he wasn't dreaming.

I didn't bother answering. Instead, I said, 'I'll make contact again as soon as we've

189

talked with her.' I was about to warn him that there were complications, none less than Tina living with a female CIA agent, a kindred spirit of our 'One-A-Month Man'. Just in time, I realized that giving him a middle-of-the-night rollercoaster ride wasn't one of my better ideas. *Leave him on a high*, I counselled myself.

We landed at JFK just before 1 a.m. and bedded down for the rest of the night at a nearby budget motel, being economic with the public purse.

Neither of us had much sleep. Our brains were tossing and turning even more than our bodies. The thrill of the chase never diminished for me. The closer I got to my quarry, the quicker the pulse of the countdown.

We didn't talk in bed, but I bet our thoughts travelled the same tramlines: what would Tina look like after all those years and cosmetic surgery? How much of her strength and vitality had been sapped and warped by the toll and toil of her past wanton life? What kind of reception would we be walking into? Would we be welcomed or would we represent ghosts of the past that she believed had been exorcized decades ago?

We were powerless to make Tina do anything against her will. Success or failure would hinge on our diplomatic adroitness. Our prospects would depend, I suspected, on how much she had confided in her partner about the dark side of her previous life.

The heartbeat of the night around JFK differed very little from its rush-hour tachycardia. The thump and throb of traffic were relentless. There was a rhythm to its drone that I found soothing; most city folk should understand that. Silence, not noise, disturbed me. For many years I'd lived under the Heathrow flight-path. And an overland ribbon of Tube lines had served as a boundary to the bottom of our backyard when I was a boy. Every time a train clattered past, the lopsided window of my mini-bedroom would vibrate, making the frame shift, almost cracking the glass. Aircraft flying overhead, either on take-off or landing, would make the whole house shudder, as if being uprooted at the epicentre of an earthquake. Those noises and disturbances would tran-quillize me more than any medication or bedtime story. It was the middle-of-the-night stillness that would wake me with a frightening start. Silence was a suffocating kind of death, where there was no pulse and the city ceased to breathe, all oxygen wrung from its lungs. But New York, like London, never needed the kiss of life. Its elixir for eternal, high-octane living came from kinetic energy. Like LA, New York lived on its nerves. Bizarrely, congestion cleared its lungs and kept it breathing. Crime and pollution killed its people, but kept it collectively alive as an entity, against all odds. The city's blocked arteries were those of a corpse, yet it ran with the constitution of a finely tuned athlete.

The faint, first light of the new day was creeping around the blinds and across the foot of the bed before I finally dozed off, only to be nudged awake by Sarah less than two hours later.

'It's six-thirty,' she said, in a wide-awake voice, devoid of early-morning phlegm. Neither of us had slept enough to be burdened by night-time debris, such as gritty eyes and dusty throats.

It was imperative that we made an early start. We showered together and were ready in half an hour for breakfast in the 1950s-styled diner that adjoined the motel. We didn't have far to drive to Queens. The previous night, we'd hired a car at the airport and a detailed street-map of the city came with the vehicle.

Tina's home was in a tree-lined avenue, where all the houses were detached, with small but neatly manicured front lawns; mostly open plan, except for a few examples of low, white picket-fencing. Each property had a double garage or car-port. Sprinklers were already hissing and spinning on a few lawns. Cars were a mix of American, European and Japanese. This was a stolid, middle-class suburb, populated by professional people. Middle everything, I guessed. Middle-aged with middle-of-the-road values and politics. Then I cautioned myself against such lazy stereotyping. Criminal history showed that this neighbourhood was the type that harboured spies and white-collar crooks, hackers and rogue City traders, and top-league fraudsters. Often a nest of vipers. Never judge a plant by its flowers. The most attractive could be the most poisonous and the same applied to people — another of my parents' homilies.

'No car in the driveway,' observed Sarah, casually; a meaningless fact, really, but it helped to maintain our concentration level.

One or two cars could have been in the garage. Although Charley had done a good job for us, there was a lot of unfinished homework. For example, we didn't have the location of the refuge that Tina ran. Neither did we know the hours she worked or whether some nights she slept at her business premises, although this was unlikely. In all probability, she employed a manageress or some kind of overseer.

The clock on the dash told us it was a couple of minutes before eight o'clock.

'The daughter should be leaving for school soon,' said Sarah.

'And Tina could be doing the school run.'

We were parked on the opposite side of the road, about fifty yards from Tina's place, a two-storey, clapboard and brick property, with a couple of slanting windows in the roof. Net curtains twitched in a couple of houses, but not in Tina's. Eyes were watching us. Jungle drums on a wavelength beyond our reach would be alerting neighbours.

'Do we have a plan?' said Sarah, aware that we didn't.

'Nope,' I said. 'Let's just play it. Last thing we want to do is rush things and blow it.'

Sarah nodded in agreement.

'I'm hoping we'll catch her alone,' I said.

'What happens if the garage opens and Tina drives out?'

'We let her drive off.'

'We don't follow?' said Sarah.

'No, we let her go. If she senses she's being followed, chances are we'll scare her. Our aim should be to put her at ease. Any case, it would be counter-productive to approach her at the refuge or any public place. We're in no hurry. We'll just wait for her to return.'

Sarah's face told me that she didn't fancy a

whole day door-stepping.

'We don't have to stay here all day,' I said, mind reading. 'We could always take in Manhattan for a few hours.' This cheered up Sarah and she switched on the radio, tuning it to an all-day music station, but keeping down the volume.

At 8.45 the garage door, electrically operated, lifted and a black Lincoln Town Car backed out. A woman was driving and a girl was belted in the front passenger-seat.

'They're coming this way,' said Sarah, as the Lincoln swung into the road, its flat, silver-grid nose pointing towards us.

Instinctively, we turned to one another, as if in intense conversation, so that the occupants of a passing car would catch only a partial snapshot of our faces. Also, hopefully, no suspicion would be aroused.

The Lincoln swept past us gracefully, but in a hurry.

'Running late,' Sarah commented.

'The big question is whether she'll return or will she go straight on to the refuge?' I said.

'Fifty-fifty.'

We had less than fifteen minutes to wait for an answer.

'Here she comes,' I reported, softly, my eyes focused on the driving mirror. 'Only one

195

person in the car.'

The driver of the Lincoln didn't even give us a casual glance in passing.

'Now what?' said Sarah.

'Let's give her five.'

The Lincoln was parked in the driveway and not returned to the garage, indicating that Tina would probably be going out again soon.

'Did you notice if there was another car in the garage when it was open for those few seconds earlier?' Sarah asked.

'I did notice and there wasn't a second car.'

'So the odds are she's now alone in the house.'

'Let's hope so,' I said. 'A couple more minutes and we'll make our move.'

Between us, there was a buoyancy that the journey's end could be in sight.

12

'Fingers crossed,' said Sarah, as we climbed from our car and strolled, as nonchalantly as possible, towards Tina's house.

The doorbell chimed musically somewhere deep in the bowels. No movement inside; no sound of approaching footsteps. Just a strange, hollow, cathedral silence.

I stepped backwards from the front door and gazed up, like a plane-spotter. A curtain shifted at the edges. Could have been caused by air-conditioning eddies, but I doubted it.

'I think we might just have been taken for Jehovah's Witnesses,' I said.

'God forbid!' said Sarah, any flippancy unintentional.

Sarah pressed the doorbell again, but wisely didn't maintain the pressure. Irking Tina would have been counter-productive.

Another wait.

More inert silence.

Another single ring of the bell, of longer duration this time, courtesy of Sarah.

Patience and reserved persistence were at last rewarded.

The intercom crackled. An articulate,

transatlantic voice said, curtly, 'Yes?'

I introduced myself via the intercom, which was as disconcerting as talking to an answer-machine. For a moment, I feared she'd been shocked into a faint. Then, piercingly, 'What do you want?'

'We're here about crimes committed long ago in the UK,' I said, deliberately vague and low-key.

More waiting. More crackling, mixed with stressed breathing.

'Who's *we?*'

'I'm Detective Sergeant Cable,' said Sarah, our English accents no doubt helping to establish our credibility.

'Do you have ID?'

'Of course,' I said.

'In that case, walk away from the front door, take out your ID and hold it above your head.'

'Anything to oblige,' I said, amused, before doing as asked.

A woman appeared framed in an upstairs window, the net curtains now around her, like a flimsy shawl. Large, military-styled binoculars were held to her eyes. After a few seconds she disappeared and, not long afterwards, the front door was opened tentatively.

'Come in,' said Tina. 'You can't be too careful, especially in my work.'

'And what is that?' I said, not wanting her to know we'd already run a comprehensive check on her.

'I help desperate women,' she said, synoptically. 'There are lots of husbands, ex-husbands, *lovers* — what a cruel misnomer — and ex-*lovers* who'd kill, literally, to get their hands around my throat.'

As soon as we were inside, she bolted the front door. Despite the house seeming to resemble all other domestic residences in the same road, this clearly was a fortress.

'Mind if we go into the kitchen?'

'Fine,' I said, following, with Sarah bringing up the rear.

'I was just having a toast-and-coffee breakfast.'

Tina had matured into a handsome, middle-aged woman, with slightly greying hair and a proud, upright bearing. She had learned to apply make-up cleverly to camouflage most of the physical scars. The kitchen was typical of an American middle-class, suburban home, fitted with every conceivable modern gadget. Tina wore lightly tinted glasses, so it was impossible to tell in which eye she was blind.

We sat on high stools around a bar-type table in the centre of the room, lit by lamp-styled lights hung low from the ceiling.

A slice of rye toast on a plate at the end of the table nearest the door had been nibbled. A half-drunk mug of black coffee beside the toast had a tepid appearance. Tina placed a mug in front of us both and poured coffee, assuming that we'd join her.

'Help yourselves to cream and sugar,' she said, pushing jug and jar towards us. Although the true mileage was recorded on her face, her classical features were still intact, but everything about her was melancholy. She could easily have been an off-duty funeral director, such was the sepulchral aura. In an about-the-house jumper, jeans and barefooted, she still looked as elegant as if dressed for a banquet. There was a quiet, understated dignity to her persona.

'So what crimes are you looking into and how can I possibly be of assistance?' Tina said, spreading herself cowgirl-fashion, as if in the saddle.

Could this be a genuine question or was she just playing a mind game? I pondered. She might have been thinking that it had something to do with her escort days and the shady characters running those kinds of agencies, but I doubted that. No, she knew. This was a charade; manoeuvring, making us earn our crust.

'Oxford, thirty-odd years ago,' I said,

momentarily leaving the rest hanging elliptically in the air.

Tina blanched.

'We have identified the perpetrator.'

'You have him in custody?' she said, astonishment etched over her face.

'No. We know who he is, though. No room for doubt.'

'Why do you need me, then?'

'Because you're a crucial witness. The one — and only one — who got away from the 'One-A-Month Man'.'

'I'm not interested,' she said, peremptorily. This was a reflex, stony statement. Absolute.

Sarah was angered, as if a barrel of gunpowder in her soul had been ignited.

'What do you mean you're not *interested?*' she flared.

Tina stared at Sarah as if firing poisoned arrows from her eyes. 'Oxford and everything therein belonged to another life of mine, before I was reborn over here. I moved on, dumping my past in the Heathrow departure lounge. I erased my first twenty years from my memory. I don't intend revisiting them — ever.'

Conveniently, she'd also erased her swinging Las Vegas days.

'Young women, your peers, fellow students with hopes and dreams, were murdered,' said

Sarah, voice and face a fire of white, pinched heat. 'They were going places in life. Going to the grave was not their choice; not why they were at Oxford. You're in the business of saving and protecting abused women, and yet you're telling us you're not *interested* in bringing to justice one of the worst abusers of women, a serial killer. Don't you feel shame?'

I flinched; Tina didn't. This was developing into a verbal skirmish between two very strong female personalities. To have come between them would have been to chance ending up as a sandwich — eaten alive by both of them.

'You've no right to sermonize to me about female responsibilities. I've paid my dues. Have you?'

Sarah eschewed being derailed. '*That* killer and abuser of women, a plunderer of futures, has been enjoying freedom for three decades, while his other victims — the bereaved families — have lived in perpetual mourning, emotionally barren, no sunshine in their lives.'

I had no idea how Tina would react. She'd be reminded of her own parents and how she abandoned them. Sarah's tirade could backfire, though it beat tacit surrender.

Tina showed signs of being winded and unbalanced by Sarah's flurry of punches.

'Tacky, mawkish sentimentality washes over me, Sergeant. You've no concept of what I've been through,' Tina said, resentfully.

'Oh, but I have. All the more reason why you should be doing somersaults at the prospect of seeing that bastard locked away for ever.'

We were trained not to show emotion. In an instant, Sarah had jettisoned all her training and conditioning; all that bureaucratic crap. She had *resorted* to behaving like a human being, like someone in the real world and not in a legislator's isolated and cocooned bubble. I was proud of her.

'I went through hell,' said Tina.

'All because of the sadism of one man, who got off on his cruel crimes.'

'I've done many things of which I'm ashamed,' Tina declared, absently.

'We know all about that, too.'

'At last I've found happiness.'

'Bully for you!'

'My partner knows nothing of my lurid past.'

'No one's concerned with what *you* did after leaving Oxford.'

'Who are you kidding? The defence would present me as a scarlet woman, someone who would say anything for a buck.'

She was right, of course.

'The prosecution would overcome that, affording you covering fire,' said Sarah, now struggling a shade, momentum stalling.

'What you're asking me to do is gamble with the life I now have. This home.' She spread her arms. 'A child. A partner. Stability. Respect.'

'If you don't do the right, honourable thing, you'll hate yourself for evermore,' Sarah prophesied, really plugging the moral high ground.

'Which pulpit did the police rescue you from?' Tina retorted, acidly.

Good question, I thought.

'Does your sanctimonious humbug really ever intimidate people?' Tina went on.

Spunky stuff.

The time had arrived, I reckoned, to make a pitch for a ceasefire.

'This man may kill again, Tina,' I said. 'For all we know, he may already have been responsible for other unsolved murders; maybe even here, in the USA.'

'*Here?* What reason have you for saying that?'

'Because he's American,' I said, 'as you'll recall.'

'He could have been Canadian,' Tina balked.

'Well, he isn't,' said Sarah, frostily.

'Does he live in the UK?' This question was asked equably.

'At present he's working there,' I explained, deliberately minimal.

'Where? In the north-east, in oil?'

'No, in London,' I said. 'He's a sort of civil servant.'

Tina's working eye widened behind the shades, her brain in top gear. 'He works for the US government?'

'Loosely,' I said, evasively.

'Then he must be based at the embassy.'

'That's something I won't be contradicting,' I said, in a long-winded way of confirming.

'Does he know you're on to him?'

'No.'

'How about his colleagues, his superiors? I assume he does have people above him and he's not the ambassador?'

'No and yes,' I said, answering the two questions in the order they were asked.

'So what does he do at the embassy?'

I hesitated. Tina didn't even know the truth about her partner working for the CIA. The last thing I wanted was to induce a conflict of interest. If Tina did agree to testify, at some stage she would have to embark on a soul-bearing and cleansing heart-to-heart with her partner. And if she announced she was giving evidence against a CIA agent, well, who knows what the ramifications and consequences might be. There was a danger that the conflicting loyalties of Tina's partner could be severely tested, turning into an emotional tug-of-war. 'I don't think I should say any more about *our man* until we're sure of your co-operation.'

Tina sank into reverie. Her toast and coffee were cold. She dismounted from her stool and poured away the dregs of her drink and binned her toast.

'Thanks for spoiling my breakfast,' she said, simultaneously checking the time with an electric clock on the wall.

'I won't say sorry because I'm not,' I said. 'I really thought you'd be heartened by the news, although, naturally, at first a little unsettled.'

Tina returned to the table desultorily and poured herself more coffee, mellowing.

'Twenty years ago I wouldn't have thought twice about it, not even bothering with a toothbrush before rushing with you to the airport. The only downside would have been that the UK had already abolished the death penalty. But now . . . now I have so much to lose. My appetite for retribution has waned. I could end up back at square one. Alone. Everything lost. I'm not sure I have the strength to begin all over again.'

'You're forgetting, Tina, that you're the innocent party, that you're the survivor, that you'll be the heroine bringing the bad guy to his well-deserved nemesis; the woman who finally unmasked the notorious 'One-A-Month Man'.'

'I need time.'

'Of course,' I said.

'If I agree to co-operate, I'll have to work out a way of bringing my partner into the loop sensitively.'

Now I simply nodded.

'Give me forty-eight hours.'

In the circumstances, it would have been unwise for us to have pushed for a tighter deadline.

'OK if we return same time in two days?' I said.

'No,' she said, emphatically. 'Give me a number and I'll call you.'

As we departed, we shook hands cordially.

★   ★   ★

'Well, what do you think?' said Sarah, as we walked purposefully away from Tina's house.

'If we were canvassers for a candidate in an election, I'd mark her down as a floating voter,' I said. 'Right now she's a pendulum, swinging to and fro.'

'The very people who decide the outcome of every election,' Sarah said.

A sobering observation. In one sense, the jury was already out on the case, long before we even had a trial.

13

As punctilious as a time-keeping obsessive, Tina called exactly forty-eight hours after we'd exited her home.

'I've given this matter very careful thought.'

Sarah used the remote to kill a TV news presenter. It also seemed to me that she'd switched off her breathing and was holding her breath.

'I decided that I had to be totally frank with my partner. We went out to dinner and I told her everything. *Really* everything. From Oxford, to LA, to Vegas, to LA, to New York. Once started, I spewed out the gut-wrenching lot. Not nice, but purging. Even therapeutic in a weird, self-flagellating way.'

I wondered about *everything*, which is infinite. Most people's *everything* is qualified; a sanitized version of an episode in life; a chapter rather than a whole book.

'We continued talking all night. We both cried. By yesterday morning, I was drained. But she was adamant. 'You *must* do it,' she said. She pledged her support, whatever it took.'

Would Tina's partner feel the same when she learned that Tina was testifying against a fellow CIA agent? But this was not the time to allow the cockroaches of doubt to feed on our feast.

I stuck up a thumb at Sarah, who performed a little celebratory tribal jig.

'So, there you have it,' Tina concluded. 'I'm in. For richer or poorer. Till death do us part!'

'I'm grateful,' I replied, which, in the circumstances, seemed so inadequate.

'I owe you an apology for the way I was the other morning. You knocked me off kilter. All kinds of thoughts ambushed me. My brain was turned into a tumble-drier. You had me in a spin. The experience was tantamount to having someone you believed was dead and buried thirty years ago turning up on your doorstep, like a ghost. A haunting.'

'No apology needed,' I said. 'I'm sure, in your shoes, I'd have reacted similarly. Worse probably.'

Her voice was no longer faltering. 'What now?'

'Good question,' I said.

Now she managed a facsimile of a titter. 'You haven't thought that far ahead, have you?'

'I'll have to take instructions,' I said, rather like a solicitor who would have to consult his client.

'Don't forget I have a daughter. She *must* be kept out of this at all costs. I'll have to make arrangements for her care well in advance of any overseas trip I have to make.'

'I'll get back to you; probably later today. When will you be home?'

'By six.'

'Call you after then,' I said.

Suddenly we were on a roll.

★　★　★

I know that this must sound risible, but I swear I heard Sharkey's heart beat like a drum-roll as I regaled him with the news.

After a few gulps, he spluttered, 'Get her on a plane. Get her over here. Don't give her time to change her mind. Keep your foot flat on the pedal. Thirty years in the wilderness! A case as cold as a maggot-eaten corpse! A medieval skeleton! Then this! It's akin to waking someone from the dead. Long dead!'

Sharkey being lyrical, albeit with a chorus of clichés, was something new. No congratulations for us, though. No 'Well done, you two! Great job!' Any glory would soon be poached. Everything had been dumped on me, but if there was a successful denouement, then the back-seat drivers would be promoting their own navigational skills. The desk-strapped Sat Navs of investigative directing would be thieving all the plaudits. As for me and Sarah, we'd be treated by the hierarchy as nothing more than reliable jobbers. Warrior material, but not cut from the cloth of chiefs.

I tried to slow him down, highlighting Tina's personal circumstances, but he wasn't listening. The only wavelength he was tuned into was his own.

'Dammit, man! That's just a matter of minor finessing,' he huffed. 'Sort it. You hear me?'

'I hear,' I said, pissed off again.

'Delicate diplomacy will be called for, involving the Home Secretary and maybe even the Foreign Office. Believe me, this is going to become a political circus.'

What he was really saying was that, as soon as we had Tina safely ensconced in the UK, the rest of the activity would be way above my salary-scale and I'd be sent packing, back to the Yard, much to Commander Pomfrey's chagrin.

* * *

Three days later, we landed at Heathrow, where Sharkey was waiting to greet us as we emerged from Arrivals. Well, that's not entirely true: he was there to ingratiate himself with Tina and to make her aware that he was the big chief who had choreographed everything and we were his mere factotums. Although I liked Sharkey, in many ways he was no different from the rest of the greasy-pole climbers. They were always on the make, always watching their backs, always with an agenda, always retaining plausible denial should anything go arse-up, and above all else, always ready to pass the buck.

We were driven to Oxford, a uniformed sergeant at the wheel, in a plush limo that came from the chief constable's executive fleet. In the two days of hectic preparations, Tina's partner had arranged for her married sister to care for Christine, Tina's daughter, in Brooklyn. We'd been invited to Tina's home for dinner, so that we could meet her partner, Laura Farrow, who was amazing. She talked endlessly, with passion, about her *work*, seemingly unaware that we knew every word was a lie. She was so immersed in her cover that she was able to discuss in enthusiastic detail the minutiae of her fabricated occupation.

Laura was much smaller and shorter than Tina; quite diminutive really. Her brunette hair was styled in a schoolboy cut and a severe fringe. She wore blood-red lipstick which made a vivid contrast with her fair, almost Goth, complexion. She had good skin and an oval, youthful face that knocked off several years from her real age. Quite easily she could have been mistaken for a thirty-five-year-old, instead of in her mid-forties. Her hair was colour-coded with her eyes and her dazzling teeth illuminated her face, lighting up her entire personality, in fact. All the time I was secretly looking for a sign of the muscle that I imagined would be essential for her dark-arts trade, but there was none visible. Her femininity seemed much more embedded than merely skin-deep. She obviously cared about her persona and was immaculately groomed. Even her jeans had been ironed and her lengthy, tapered fingernails were varnished to complement her lips. Through the eyes of a man, she had a body that stirred the libido. Even the fact that she was a lesbian did nothing to dilute my testosterone.

The evening had been both convivial and enlightening; a lesson in how convincingly a spook could live a lie, believing it to such an extent that it was far more real to Laura than any conventional virtual reality.

★ ★ ★

Sharkey had booked Tina into the Holiday Inn on the northern periphery of Oxford. Unbridled as ever, he hoped to elicit a statement from her the moment we reached *his* city, but Tina was bushed and couldn't resist any longer the pull of gravity to the bed. For Tina this was coming home for the first time since she'd fled, hoping to shed all the warts and scars that had disfigured her reputation after her unscheduled encounter with the 'One-A-Month Man', sending her life into a nosedive.

Neither I nor Sarah appreciated the enormity of this home-coming for Tina. Not once so far had she asked about her parents. I doubted that she even knew her father had committed suicide. Perhaps she was too scared of the answers to ask the questions. I couldn't believe that she didn't care, not deep down, not in her core, however much she'd craved for a blank canvas on which to start redrawing her life so long ago.

On that drive from Heathrow to Oxford, even though so obviously mentally exhausted, she didn't once shut her eyes; it was as if she was seeing England for the first time. Small fields. Neat hedgerows. Country lanes. Quaint pubs. Thatched cottages. All vehicles driving on the left-hand side of the road. There was a schoolgirl's awe to her

215

kaleidoscope of expressions, changing with the regularity of traffic lights. Self-induced amnesia may have been an integral part of her past survival kit.

As we neared the hotel, there was a signpost displaying the mileage to Bedford, Tina's home town, but, if she saw it, no visible impact was reflected on her tired, gaunt face or in her one working eye.

Certain basic arrangements had been put in place before our arrival. A uniformed sentinel would be on guard outside Tina's bedroom throughout every night and Tina was never to be left alone during the day. Sharkey had planned for her to be chaperoned by one of his own female detective constables, believing that Sarah and I were now redundant, but Tina would have none of it.

'I'm here because of these two,' Tina told Sharkey, alluding to me and Sarah. 'I trust them. If they go, I go — back to New York.'

Sharkey, sensibly, caved in without protest. 'If that's the way you want it, that's fine by me. I hadn't realized the three of you had become such bosom pals, so inseparable.'

His little dig didn't make even the tiniest of dents in Tina's resolve.

So we stayed on the case. We were provided with a room next to Tina's and now Sharkey

216

made no moral judgment because, by sharing, we were saving his force money. When it came to money or morality, no contest.

On the second day of Tina's stay in Oxford, we drove her mid-morning to the city-centre police station, where we took a statement from her, amounting to a tome, which we later had sworn as an affidavit. We lunched at a desk on a selection of sandwiches, bottled water and copious coffee. We didn't finish until gone five, by which time Tina's eyelids were already drooping again.

'Thank God that's over!' said Tina, yawning.

I refrained from replying, 'This isn't even the beginning,' which would have been the daunting truth.

As soon as I was with Sharkey, behind the soundproof glass of his sanctuary, he said, 'OK, now we're in business. First thing in the morning, I'm off to London to talk with people at the Yard and Home Office to formulate tactics. We've got to get this right. When you get a big fish on the end of a line, you can so easily lose it by trying to reel it in too fast. Slowly does it! Don't let *that* woman out of your sight.'

He was dazzled by images of a commendation, promotion, and even a knighthood.

Nothing was more seductive than the come-hither temptress promising glory and adulation.

During dinner at the hotel, Sarah popped the question, as a statement, that had been lurking in my head for so long.

'Being in Oxford again, Tina, must bring back so many memories for you.'

Tina averted her eye, which had moistened. Suddenly her appetite evaporated. The tips of her fingers trembled and a string of sweat-pearls appeared strung across her forehead.

'Not many good memories,' she said, dismally, after an expanded deliberation. And then, 'How much do you know of my history? I don't mean just about my Oxford days. My life has been divided into segments and in each of them I've been a different person.' Wistfully, she continued, 'Before I came here, to university, I was so carefree, so happy, so emotionally immature, so genuinely innocent.'

'Weren't you ever happy here?' said Sarah, feeding Tina's melancholic self-analysis.

'Oh, yes. I was having a ball. Until . . . until *that* night. Then I grew up in just a few seconds. The halcyon days were over. Instead, I discovered what the *real* world was like; the barbaric world of men.'

Now her eye was a reptilian mirror of the viperous poison that she harboured for my gender. Earlier she'd told Sharkey how much she trusted *us*, packaging me with Sarah, yet I represented the enemy, the target of her long-festering hostility. There was confliction here, but that was to be expected considering all the turbulence she'd been buffeted by since her path became a collision course with the 'One-A-Month' killer. Inconsistency was her right.

'I've talked at length with your mother,' I said, catching her off-guard.

Instantly her face belonged to someone on the wrong end of an unfair blow below the belt.

'My mum?' she stammered, like an adult orphan being reminded that she once had a biological mother and had not come out of a test-tube. 'So she's still alive?' There was something truly caring and womb-orientated about this question.

'I'd say that she's been sustained all these years by the hope, however forlorn, of one day being reunited with you.'

Tina was hit hard and it hurt. 'I was so unbelievably messed up,' she said, trying to explain the inexplicable, her tone apologetic and self-recriminating.

'I'm sure your parents would have

understood,' said Sarah, sympathetically.

'I don't see how they would because I didn't understand myself. I needed to escape from everything by which I was identified. If I could have shed my skin, I would have done so gladly. I was literally cutting myself loose from all the labels of my life.'

'Didn't you ever have the urge to pick up the phone and call home, if only to say, 'Don't worry, I'm OK'?' said Sarah, a shade critically.

'A million times, but the longer I put it off, the harder it became. I kept leaving it until it was too late; the gap was too wide to bridge, or so I thought. My father actually tracked me down on one occasion; did you know that?'

'We do,' I said.

'What could I say to them after that? Can you imagine the embarrassment? You've seen the sort of home I grew up in. You've seen my parents: church-going, God-fearing, middle-class, stereotype bourgeoisie.'

'I didn't have the opportunity to meet your father,' I said, sparsely, giving Tina a cue.

'He must have retired some years ago.'

'I'm afraid he threw himself in front of an express train, shortly after his abortive encounter in London with you,' I said, bluntly, turning the screw.

Genuinely horror-struck, her face contorted by grief and self-loathing, she said, 'Oh my God! Dad was always so stoical; a backbone-of-Britain type. Nothing ever fazed him. He was the sort of man you'd want on an aircraft in an emergency. He'd soak up all the panic and replace it with calm serenity. What have I done? What my poor mother must have been through! And all because of me.' I didn't detect any self-pity. 'How can anyone ever make up for all the misery I've generated?'

'You can't,' I said, harshly. The brutal truth was better than a cheap, anodyne lie.

'But doing the right thing now, which you are, will go a long way towards balancing the books,' Sarah quickly pitched in, dousing any flames, instead of fanning them, for which I was renowned.

Tina used her serviette to mop up her tears. 'Would I be welcome in my mother's home now, do you suppose?' she asked, hesitantly and rhetorically.

'A reunion would complete the circle of your mother's life, I'm certain of that,' said Sarah, playing the good fairy.

'Is she still living in the same house, my childhood home?'

'Same one,' I said.

For a few moments, a sort of hallowed and

sepulchral silence enveloped us, as if we had just entered a holy building, a temple, whereupon all conversations were guillotined, even those in mid-sentence.

'We could always act as a conduit for you,' suggested Sarah, looking to me for support.

'No problem,' I said.

'Would you *really?*'

'Really,' I reaffirmed.

'I need time to prepare myself.'

'Time is the one thing you should have in abundance for the next few days,' I said.

We retired to our rooms together. A uniformed officer, semi-automatic slung over his shoulder, was sitting outside the door to Tina's room, a soft porn magazine tucked down the side of the chair. He nodded to me as Tina let herself into her room, the door clicking closed behind her, immediately followed by the sound of the bolt being applied and the security chain fastened.

'Have you ever had to use that thing?' I asked, conversationally, gesturing towards the weapon.

'Twice. Kid bicycle-thieves. Separate occasions. Got 'em point-blank. In the back of the head. Dead in an instant. Brains made a mess of the bikes.'

'What!' I exclaimed, aghast, at first missing his piss-taking grin.

'But only in my meanest dreams,' he added, slyly.

Secretly, he must have been saying to himself, *Gotcha, stupid big-shot!*

* ★ ★ ★

Tina's reunion with her mother was set up by Sarah. I wanted no part of it. Although I was invited along as chauffeur, I declined emphatically. A tea party for a prodigal daughter, accompanied by a feast of cloying, mawkish sentimentality, was not my idea of a joy-ride.

While they were in Bedford, the news came through to me, via one of Sharkey's acolytes, that a warrant had been issued for the arrest of Richard Pope. The plan was to charge him with the three murders and the assault of Tina with intent to murder.

'Who will be making the arrest?' I asked.

The cough that preceded his answer was a mannerism, like a nervous tic. 'Me, of course. Only right that I should. Protocol, that's all.'

'So if there's a cock-up, the fallout lands on your head and shoulders, right?'

Glory-hunters have to live by the same rules as head-hunters. Sometimes it's their heads that end up scalped.

'I have broad shoulders,' he boasted.

'I'll remind you of that, if need be,' I warned.

A chill was developing in the air between us.

'I'll be returning to Oxford tomorrow, but I don't know when. In the meantime, don't let our queen bee witness out of your sight.'

I think if I'd disclosed to Sharkey that Tina and Sarah had gone to Bedford, leaving me in Oxford, the only arrest impacting on his life would have been a cardiac one.

'I'll keep you updated,' he said, his way of signing off.

* * *

Sarah called me around eight in the evening. 'We'll be on the road in about five,' she said, straight to the point.

'How did it go?'

'There were so many tears I feared the three of us would be drowned.'

'Lived up to my expectations, then. I've always been a poor swimmer in emotional floods. Keeping well away from it was a good call of mine.'

'Tina's mum's on cloud nine, still walking on air.'

'That beats walking on water,' I said. 'Who said modern miracles lacked biblical panache?'

'Obviously not you.'

Next morning, we killed time. While the women went to the indoor swimming pool, I worked out in the gym. Late afternoon, I took Sharkey's second call of the day. Right from the outset I knew that all was not well.

'Negotiations have been initiated with US ambassadorial staff,' he stated, flatly.

'Amicable?'

'Oh, yeah.' There was something sardonic in his voice now.

'No problem, then, about a handover?'

'Oh, yeah; one very big problem. The Home Office has been informed that there's no Richard Pope based at the US Embassy. He doesn't exist. Our 'One-A-Month Man' is a phantom. Figment of the imagination.'

I was left contemplating Sharkey's broad shoulders.

14

A depression had descended over Oxford; well, over our little quarter of the cloistered city.

Three long faces.

Not a smile for a mile.

Sharkey hadn't shaved. I hadn't slept. Sarah hadn't bothered with a comb or hairbrush.

We sat around a bare-topped table in the briefing room. Sharkey assumed the role of chairman of the board. Our demeanours and appearances accurately mirrored the collective mood. Morose and crestfallen.

'We're being stitched up,' said Sharkey.

'Obviously,' I said.

'Where's the fucking coffee?' Sharkey growled, digressing and thumping the table with a hairy fist. There was passion in his punch. In his mind's eye, I sensed he was punching to splinter human bone and tissue, rather than wood.

On cue, a rap on the door heralded the arrival of three coffees, in ghastly polystyrene mugs, courtesy of a harassed, uniformed female rookie.

Sharkey's appreciation was restricted to a grunt.

The coffee-bearing officer's antennae didn't need to be very sensitive in order to pick up the vibes. Sensibly, she beat a hasty, muted retreat.

'He's *in* there!' Sharkey boomed, again underscoring his assertion with knuckle on wood.

'Are you accusing the US ambassador of being a liar, of orchestrating a conspiracy to obstruct justice?' said Sarah, her temerity evoking a look from Sharkey suggesting that he'd just spied a cockroach swimming in his drink.

'Stuff the semantics!' he seethed. 'What I'm *saying* — not fucking *suggesting* — is that we're being shat on from high.'

'Don't all embassies have to list their diplomatic staff to the appropriate agencies of host countries?' I said, prosaically, hoping to lower temperature and tension.

'Of course they bloody do! Of course they're bloody *meant* to.'

'So what's the Foreign Office say?' said Sarah, not the least cowed by Sharkey's petulance.

'Richard Pope entered the UK at Heathrow nineteen months ago to be a part of the US embassy establishment in London. This is confirmed by M15. Our Intelligence people know about everyone at all the embassies in the capital. They know who are the legits and who are the spooks.'

'Might it not be a simple matter of Pope being on leave?' said Sarah.

'The only *simple* fact in all this is that we're being farted on — from a great height and with an equally great blast,' said Sharkey, unrelenting with his vitriol. 'No, it's not a *simple matter* of his being on leave. The message was categorical: there's no Richard Pope on the US Embassy's books in London.'

'They can't deny that he entered the UK and was on the embassy payroll,' I said, perplexed.

'They haven't tried to. They're being typically duplicitous and vague. By *typically*, I mean fork-tongued, cloak-and-dagger, diplomatic lizards. Shysters all!'

'Is Pope known to our Intelligence agencies as a CIA operative?' I asked.

'Yes.'

'If he's been repatriated, wouldn't our people have to be informed?' I continued.

'Of course. A matter of protocol.'

'And that hasn't happened?' said Sarah.

'No.'

'Has he accommodation in the embassy or has he been living elsewhere?' I said.

'If he lived outside the embassy, arresting him would have been easy. No, he's holed up in *there*, his sanctuary, a bolt-hole, like a church in medieval times, where he can't be

228

bagged by us. While in the embassy, he's on US soil, governed by US legislation. Diplomatic immunity! Diplomatic impunity, I call it! The bane of *our* lives.'

'But the moment he steps outside, he's all ours,' I said, not with a great amount of optimism, I must confess.

'In theory,' said Sharkey, still doleful. 'But we don't even know what he looks like nowadays. We have photos of him as a student, but that was all of thirty years ago. He could be fat, bald, bespectacled, and sporting a Father Christmas beard, for all we know.'

'Surely MI5 will have an up-to-date mug-shot of him on file,' I said.

'That's a thought,' said Sharkey, perking up a little. 'But it's still not going to get us far unless there's a thaw in Grosvenor Square and a deal is brokered. Scotland Yard won't be able to watch the embassy day and night for us indefinitely, just in case Pope should sneak out, even if they have a current photo of him. We're well and truly stymied, that's the bottom line.' The gloom had returned.

'Seems to me all you can do is keep pressing,' I said.

Then to an issue that couldn't be eschewed. 'What shall I tell Tina?'

Emblematic of a pilloried brain, Sharkey thrummed his podgy fingers on the table.

'What a cock-up! But as things are, we can't justify keeping her here any longer, funding her stay from the public purse. We're going to have to let her go.'

'There's no guarantee she'll be prepared to return,' I cautioned.

'So be it,' said Sharkey, throwing up his hands in surrender, a hostage to his force's budget. 'For all I know, we could be at a permanent impasse. Break it to her gently. Try to keep her sweet, just in case.'

The meeting was over. Career-wise, this had to be my nadir. Success, so quickly, had turned sour.

★　★　★

As we drove to the hotel, in tomb-like silence, an idea was already germinating in my head, but I decided not to share it with Sarah just yet. Give it time to crystallize.

Tina had remained in her room, with a female chaperone from Sharkey's stable deputizing for Sarah and an armed guard in the corridor.

'That was quick,' said Tina. 'I was expecting you to be gone most of the day. Something wrong?'

She looked from me to Sarah and back again.

'We need to talk,' I said, solemnly. 'Alone.'

Sarah's stand-in took the hint, saying, 'I'll be off, then. Plenty for me to get on with elsewhere.'

There was no way of softening what I had to tell Tina. A doctor had once said to me, 'If a patient has terminal cancer, you can't package the news in tinsel, as if it's a Christmas present at the top of a wish-list. The kindest way to deliver the blow is straight to the chin, but with a padded glove. 'The bad news is that you're going to die; the good news is that, with luck, it won't be today.''

So I followed the good doctor's prescription. I told Tina everything about Pope and his role with the US government and what he was doing in London, and the outcome of negotiations to have him handed over. When I'd finished, Tina said, subdued, 'So they're closing ranks?'

'Looks that way,' I said.

She was sitting deflated on the side of the bed, head in her chest. I was squatting on the writing desk, alongside the TV, while Sarah stood at the window, a silhouette the other side of the net curtain, her back to us, staring into space.

Tina glanced at the subtle green glow of crystal digits at the foot of the blank TV screen. I realized what she was doing:

231

converting UK time from the screen clock into New York time.

'There's no chance of Laura being at home yet,' she said, as if dictating a memo to herself. 'I'll fly home tomorrow. Can you book me on a flight?'

'Of course,' said Sarah, swivelling away from the window, unravelling herself from the hanging veil. 'Leave it to me.'

We'd bought Tina an 'open' return ticket in New York as our last waltz in the dance of diplomacy to secure her agreement. Now she just wanted a quick-step out of Oxford.

Oxford had given her a raw deal as a student. Nothing had changed for her. She would call her mother to say farewell, no doubt appreciating that it would also be a final goodbye, a fact that would not be lost on Mrs Marlowe.

Machinations were scuttling around inside my head. With luck I could manipulate a window of opportunity with a time-frame of perhaps three hours, which I would definitely need.

'We'll only be kicking our heels until tomorrow, so if you want to fit in some last-day shopping, I'm sure Sarah would be happy to keep you company,' I said, conjuring up nonchalance.

Sarah shot me a look that screamed, *Now*

what are you up to?

'Might as well,' Tina said, lethargically. 'I ought to get something for Laura. She always brings me back a little pressie every time she's been on a trip. She's very thoughtful that way.' Finally, lifting her head and spirits, she said to Sarah, 'I'm ready whenever you are.'

'Take your time,' I said, provoking yet another searching look from Sarah.

I went down to the lobby with them and watched them drive away from the car park before making a call to my favourite *mechanic* at the Yard.

'You busy?' I said.

'Always am, seven/seven.'

'Fancy dropping everything to do me a favour?'

'Depends where and what. *Dropping everything* isn't the kind of open cheque I'll ever sign — you should know that.'

Succinctly, I briefed her of my requirements.

'Sounds straightforward enough,' she said. 'Shouldn't take me more than five minutes once I'm with you.'

'That really is a quickie, but you'll need to get here pronto to avoid being caught in the act. A three-hour time-frame at the most.'

'That's OK. I'm wearing my wings today.'

233

'Just burn rubber,' I said.

'For you, duckie, I'd burn my bra.'

★ ★ ★

Detective Constable Maggie Diamond, the hotshot *mechanic*, had only marginally overstated her expertise.

Her prophesy that she'd be 'in and out' within five minutes was only a trifle over-optimistic. I marvelled at her deft, sleight-of-hand skill, almost amounting to sorcery.

'All done,' she announced, slapping generous hips trapped inside tailored jeans.

After we'd exited Tina's room, we walked together to Maggie's BMW sports car, a present from her dad, a Harley Street forensic psychiatrist, who was often employed by prosecution and defence counsels as an expert witness in court cases.

'You're *au fait* with the equipment, aren't you?' she said, just as she was hoisting herself behind the wheel.

'If I'm not by now, I never shall be,' I said, when 'yes' would have been sufficient and more economic.

'It shouldn't let you down because it's foolproof,' she said, her eyes sparkling with innuendo.

'Obviously made with me in mind, then,' I quipped, relying on self-deprecation to keep me in the joust.

'Incidentally, there's no chance of my burning a bra for you now because I'm not wearing one,' she said, as a punchline.

'Now you tell me!' I rejoined.

She grinned, gunned the engine, and was gone, with a throaty roar.

The red-eyed tail of Maggie's BMW had only just filtered into the main highway traffic when Sarah's car nosed sedately, by contrast, into the car park.

Instead of hanging around to greet them, I hotfooted my way to my room to prepare to operate the high-tech equipment that Maggie had installed.

As I lay on the bed, propped up by a bank of pillows, I heard Tina letting herself into her room. I recognized Sarah's voice, but I couldn't make out more than a few random words: 'See you later . . . after a shower . . . ' Something was said about having a rest and meeting for an early dinner. The door to Tina's room closed and the security chain went on.

Seconds later, Sarah tapped on our door. 'Use your key,' I called out. 'It's not bolted.'

As she stepped across the threshold, she froze. 'What the hell are you doing?' she demanded, ploughman's furrows coursing across her fore-head.

'Shush!' I hissed, a finger pressed against my mouth.

Her eyes followed the flex from my earphones, down the bed, across the floor to the limpet mike that gripped the wall, held firm by suction.

Now Sarah knew exactly what was happening. After slipping out of her boots, she tiptoed towards me.

'She won't be making a call to Laura until after dinner,' Sarah whispered. 'But I don't see what you're hoping to glean from it.'

'You'll see.'

★   ★   ★

The three of us dined together at seven. There was little conversation. Tina ate little, while I tucked into three courses. Sarah could tell that I was on another high, but her appetite was little better than Tina's. We were back into our rooms by 8.30.

The limpet mike allowed me to hear and record every sound from within Tina's room. Her TV was murmuring on low. 'I think she's packing,' I said. Then, a bit later, 'Now she's taking a shower.' Sarah, lying on the bed reading a magazine, widened her eyes in a sardonic, *Wow! What excitement* response.

Sarah was dozing and I was struggling to keep open my eyes, when I heard Tina start to punch out a number on her bedside phone. The time was midnight: 7p.m. in New York.

A connection was made. 'Laura, it's me.'

Of course I could hear only Tina's end of the conversation, but I was gambling on that being adequate.

'*I wasn't sure if you'd be home . . . How's my darling daughter? That's a relief! . . . Isn't she pining just a wee bit for her mom?* (hope in her voice) *. . . Oh, well, that's kids for you* (disappointment) *. . . Puts us adults in our place, doesn't it? We're deluding ourselves when we think we're indispensable to them . . . No, I'm not feeling sorry for myself; that's a lie, of course . . . Nevertheless, I am on a real downer . . . Why? I'll tell you why: everything's gone pear-shaped. It's not the cops' fault, no blame on the Brits. It's those bastards at our embassy in London . . . Yes, the US embassy — that's where the shit's based. But they're pretending he's not there . . . Never heard of the guy! All that crap . . .*

'*What am I going to do? I'm coming home and sod it! . . . Yes, tomorrow . . . A morning flight, I think. I'll let you know . . . Oh, yes, they've treated me very well, like royalty; I've*

237

no complaint on that score, but I'm regretting having got enmeshed in all this. It's been so unsettling and all for nothing. All those nightmare memories I'd finally managed to bury have been resurrected. I've had my nightmares here: like being at the movies and forced to watch scenes of what I went through all those years ago, and then the realization hits me that I'm back in the city where it happened. It's been so surreal.

'I never again want to hear the name Richard Pope . . . I mean, of all things, he's with the CIA; can you believe that? . . . Yes, CIA, that's what I said. I wish the cops had let me into that little secret when they were in New York. I might have had second thoughts about getting involved. I don't fancy tangling with those cowboys. If I'd known, I could have told Lorenzo that he was beating his head against a brick wall . . . No way will that bunch hand HIM over. HE's bound to know too much about their black ops for them to allow him to be interrogated in open court . . . Yes, his name is Richard Pope — as in the Vatican. His old man, dead now, used to be big in politics, a Democrat, a string-puller . . . Probably a whole family of string-pullers.

'There has to be a smarter game-plan than taking on the Ivy League hard-balls . . . I don't know what to believe . . . If he was in

238

the embassy, you can bet your life they've spirited him away by now . . . What do you mean to look after myself and watch my back? There's a cop with a machine-gun outside my room every minute of the day and night, and whenever I go out I'm shadowed by Sarah or Mike or both of them. This is life in a straightjacket, so stop worrying. I'll be home tomorrow. Will you be able to meet me? Oh, that's good. I should be on a mid-morning flight. If that's the case, I'll probably be at JFK around 2 p.m., but I'll give you my exact itinerary later.

'Are you likely to be making a trip soon? Oh, that's a shame. It would have been nice to have a few days together, but work is money and money is survival. See you tomorrow.'

Tina blew a couple of kisses into the phone.

'So how was that, Mr Snoopy?' said Sarah, who was now sitting upright. Alert. Fully switched on.

'Perfect.'

'Been turned on by dirty talk?'

'No dirty talk. Very loving and solicitous, as a matter of fact.'

'So what have you learned?'

'Nothing . . . and everything.'

Her face once more was creased with

curiosity. 'Yet you implied that you got all that you were listening for; that your eavesdropping paid off.'

'So it did.'

'You're losing me.'

'Good; getting one over on you is so rare it's worth celebrating.'

'What have you in mind?'

'Come closer and I'll show you.'

She did and I revealed all. She, too.

15

After *celebrating* between the sheets, we remained tangled, like a pair of exhausted wrestlers who had agreed to a truce.

We talked endlessly. When a man and a woman are naked together, it's easy — mandatory, in fact — to bare all. A couple of puzzles still nagged me: one revolved around how Tina and Laura became an item. I asked Sarah if, during their shopping excursion and other times alone, this subject had ever been touched upon.

'They met in a Manhattan gay bar,' said Sarah. 'Became friends. Started seeing one another regularly. It went from there, same as any other relationship, Mike. No great mystery.'

'Surely the CIA would have got to know about it?'

'So what, Mike? Since when have you been homophobic?'

'Never, but . . . ' I stumbled along.

'We have gay cops, don't we? Very useful for working the gay scene undercover when necessary. Same would apply to the CIA, surely?'

'You're right,' I caved in. 'What explanation did she give to Laura about losing her sight in one eye?'

'The truth. Well, half-truth. A jealous lover. A little light on detail, until we came along and she spilled everything.'

'Something else has bothered me,' I said, sort of enigmatically.

'OK, let's hear it.' She spoke like a wife about to be accused by her husband of having an affair.

'Just think about Tina's history.'

'A lot to think about,' she said. 'Which particular clip?'

'Her messing around with Sergi Chekov. I mean, she actually married the guy! Because so much has happened, we're forgetting that she meddled with espionage.'

'*I* hadn't forgotten. What's your point?'

'The FBI was tipped off about her. They'd have kept tabs on her. And when she teamed up with Laura they'd have suspected that she was up to her old tricks and was a national security risk. At the very least, Laura would have been warned off. Get me?'

'I *get* you, but I think you're forgetting how the world has changed.'

'Oh, really?' I said, a shade defensively.

'Yes, *really*! Sergi was a Soviet. The Cold War was just thawing, but Tina's *activities*

242

with Sergi were solely Russian-based. The Americans would have labelled her a Communist-sympathizer. A baddie. But then the Berlin Wall and Iron Curtain came down. Democracy was embraced. The Soviet Union split up. Elections were introduced. And all international attention began to focus on the Middle East, with the emergence of the Taliban and Al Qaeda. After 9/11, do you think the FBI and indeed any of the West's Intelligence agencies would have been the least concerned about a long-time-ago, clapped-out honeypot from the UK?'

'That's a bit harsh,' I said, 'calling Tina clapped out.'

'Well, she is, in the context of seduction. Powerful men who can be choosy wouldn't be panting after one-eyed, acid-stained Tina, now would they?'

'God, you're so poetic!'

'And plausible?'

'Probably,' I said.

★ ★ ★

Sex was over for the night. My recovery rate was slower than Sarah's, my libido always lagging behind hers by several hours. Too much boozing in the past had caused ironical and conflicting damage: hardened liver and

243

softened organ. That's life for you; nature had a wicked way of making punishment fit the crime.

Although I no longer boozed, I still suffered hangovers. Sexual hangovers. When I woke — that's assuming my metabolism had slowed sufficiently to allow me some sleep — I'd feel as dehydrated and liverish as if I'd had a skinful of alcohol, rather than the even more potent juices of carnality.

Naturally, our talk gravitated towards the comparatively mundane matters of work, the subject that bridged the chasm between two very different personalities and psyches. If we hadn't both been cops, we'd never have been drawn to one another. Sarah would have been in the bed of someone far more worthy. I might still have been with my wife and family. More likely, though, I'd have been in a bar, digging my grave, making a down-payment towards my funeral.

'Come clean . . . '

'Unfortunate choice of words,' I cut her short.

She giggled contentedly and snuggled even closer and deeper.

'It's time to clean up your act,' she admonished me, playfully. 'Be serious. Where do we go from here?'

'To sleep, hopefully,' I replied, obstructively.

244

'And then?'

'We go with Tina.'

Instantly, I sensed her sweaty body tense up. She tilted back her head so that she had my face sharply in focus. 'To New York?'

'That's where she'll be flying to, isn't it?'

'But why do *we* go?'

'Because she's going to lead us to Pope.'

Now she broke loose from me, immediately sobering up from sexual inebriation. 'How? You're not *seriously* suggesting she knows his whereabouts?'

'Of course not. I'm sure the US ambassador and his underlings in London haven't been lying when maintaining that Pope's not with them. It's the truth, but not the whole truth. He *was* there, of that I have no doubt, but he's been posted elsewhere. Spirited away. A rush job; the moment approaches were made to them through diplomatic channels. That's my take on it.'

'Yet, apparently, there's no evidence of his being on any flight passenger list out of the UK.'

'You're not *that* naïve, Sarah. *Those* people have briefcases stuffed with passports in different names and nationalities. He could even have been flown in a private jet from a rural air strip to any European country, where he connected with a scheduled flight to a US city.'

'Accepted. But that doesn't answer how Tina might know where he's flown.'

'You're right. She won't have a clue, but Laura Farrow will. Right now, I guarantee, Laura is in a networking frenzy. By the time Tina lands in New York, Laura will have chapter and verse of Pope's disappearing act.'

'How far have you thought this through?' she said, mental battery now fully recharged.

'Far enough.'

'But Mike, we're finished on this case,' she said, exasperated. 'We'll be heading for London tomorrow, not New York.' With a reflex twist of her head, she examined her wristwatch. 'I should have said *today*, not *tomorrow*.' The time was a shade after 1 a.m. and sleep was obviously still a long way off.

'I've booked the three of us on a noon flight from Heathrow,' I stated, doggedly. 'Paid for with my Yard credit card, so Sharkey's force won't be footing one penny of the bill.'

'That's possibly even worse! Pomfrey will combust. We'll both be on garden leave.'

'Not if we nail Pope.'

'It's a gamble, Mike. You're deluding yourself, but not me.'

'Dedication not delusion,' I retaliated, prickly.

'You've an unparalleled track record of

punting on losers with pocket-emptying regularity,' she said cruelly, though somewhat truthfully. 'Now you're backing yet another wild, irresponsible hunch. If you were proposing following a lead to Newcastle, fair game, but to New York! We'll be accused of splashing out public money on a luxury junket.'

'Pomfrey will be delighted to have me off his radar for a few more days.'

'No, no, Mike. He'll see it as a chance to get you out of his hair for ever. You'll get the boot. And you'll take me down with you.'

'Ultimate togetherness!' I said. 'Embracing as we drown. Romantic, don't you think?'

'*Titanic* togetherness! What's romantic about that? I'm in no mood for a suicide pact.'

'We could even take off without informing either Sharkey or Pomfrey,' I said, my elbow deployed as a fulcrum on the mattress as I faced Sarah, my legs under the covers and my torso, still a suffusion of sweat, above the plimsoll line, cooling off.

Now Sarah eyed me snake-like, as if I really had flipped.

'You're serious, aren't you?'

'Never been more so.'

'And you expect me to go along with you, over the cliff edge, like a lemming?'

'I can't see you chickening out.'

'Mike, this isn't the occasion for a school kid's prank or chest-beating virility test.'

'I'll tell you what it is, though, Sarah: it's the one and only chance we'll have to make a catch. There's no pressure on you from me. If you want out, that's your prerogative. I'll be disappointed, but I'll go it alone.'

'What do you mean there's *no pressure* on me? Of course there is and you damn well know it. You may not intend moral blackmail, but that's what it amounts to.'

'Only in your own head, Sarah.'

'What you're proposing is madness, Mike. Putting a gun to your head and pulling the trigger. One bullet for both of us.'

'Is that your final verdict?'

'Yes, absolutely, irreversibly final.'

Ten hours later, Sarah and Tina were with me at Heathrow, the three of us boarding a New York-bound flight.

★　★　★

Tina was pleased to have our company on the flight, of course, and assumed we were there for her protection.

'Will you have to return to London as soon as you've seen me safely collected?' she said, after a couple of hours into the transatlantic flight.

248

'Probably,' I said. 'We'll have to await instructions.'

'You're very welcome to stay with me and Laura until you're recalled,' she offered. 'I want to dive back into the deep end of work as soon as possible, but my home can be yours for a few days while you rest up.'

I thanked her for her generosity, but declined as graciously as possible, saying that it was almost certain that we'd be winging our way homeward bound that same evening, doubling up on jet-lag.

'Poor things,' she said, her sympathy seemingly genuine.

Laura was in the Arrivals Hall, teetering anxiously, peering over heads as all the passengers from our flight — and several others that had landed around the same time — spewed from Customs like water gushing from a burst main. She waved frantically and called out the moment she spied Tina.

Laura and Tina hugged one another as if they'd been parted for years; Tina, a warrior, returning from a war-zone, thankfully not in a body-bag, not even wounded: it was that kind of 'tie a yellow ribbon' homecoming. They kissed, just the once, while Sarah and I discreetly allowed our attention to be diverted.

Tina explained to Laura that we wouldn't be going any further with them, but Laura insisted that we at least had a drink with them at the airport, so we migrated, rather desultorily, to one of the self-service cafeterias, where we perched on high stools at a shelf eating-surface against a wall, beneath a monitor that listed flight departure and arrival details, updated every few seconds.

'I must thank you for all your efforts and I know that you must be as gutted as Tina,' Laura said, solemnly. 'Now the most important thing for Tina is that she's able to put this behind her as quickly as possible and, hopefully, can slip back seamlessly into the life from which she was uprooted. Rightfully uprooted, I acknowledge. She had to do it, but now it's all over. In life you have to learn when to cut your losses. That beast Pope was out of Tina's cognition for thirty years. You reintroduced him into her life, but now he's gone again and that's how it must remain, if only for Tina's sanity. Gone for ever!'

God, this woman was good! I looked into her eyes and she could have been giving the Sermon on the Mount, so much pained sincerity hanging over her like a halo. She was all heart, yet it was a slick sham; tantamount to a politician's vote-seducing rhetoric. If she had a weakness, it was vanity. It's one thing to be a smart operator, but to know it and to indulge yourself is risky. Humility and even a modicum of self-doubt made better armour and camouflage than over-confidence, something to which I could testify from painful experience. I'd paid the full price, without any discount.

'How soon will you be on your travels?' Tina said to Laura, conversationally, not excluding us.

'Tomorrow, I'm afraid. First thing.' The sadness in Laura's voice was at odds with the excitement and eagerness in her eyes.

'Where to this time?' Tina enquired, heavy-hearted, shoulders sagging, eyes dull. 'Out of town or out of country?'

I could read in Sarah's face that she suspected me of having primed Tina to ask these questions, but I hadn't.

'Out of country. How are your nerves? Will you be OK while I'm gone?'

'Of course I'll be OK,' Tina replied, almost snappily. 'It's not as if I can't take care of myself and I'll have my daughter home with me. I'll collect her this evening.'

'She'll be pleased you're home,' Laura said, soothingly.

'Any idea how long you'll be away?'

'Hopefully, only a few days — three or four at a stretch.'

'You still haven't said *exactly* where you're going?'

'Nassau. Sunny Bahamas.'

'How my heart bleeds for you!' said Tina, her envy contrived. Then a quick change of pace and direction, 'No problem at the refuge?'

'Not that I've heard; no cries for help.'

'Bad taste!' said Tina, reprovingly.

'I meant no panic from staff,' Laura explained herself, evenly.

'Look, I think we should get on,' I said, unhooking myself from my stool and kick-starting the valedictory handshaking ritual, with Sarah copying.

Tina and Laura both stood. 'You did your best, I know that,' said Tina, running a finger down my arm. 'The odds were stacked against us.' She kissed me on the cheek. 'You're both going to be so bushed when you hit London again.'

'No different from a hangover,' I observed, lightening the mood.

'Something Mike has a head for!' said Sarah, eliciting polite but mirthless smiles.

As we crossed the concourse, Sarah said, earnestly now, 'Do you believe Laura's destination is the Bahamas?'

'Don't know. Doubt it. Depends what game she's playing.'

'What next for us?'

'We keep out of sight for an hour or so

until we're sure they've gone, then return to this concourse to hire a car.'

'And after that, where do we spend the night?'

'In the car, near their home, but not *too* near. Laura could be flying from any of three airports: JFK, LaGuardia or New Jersey. We have to be certain which one, so we'll need to tail, without being made.'

'My, Mike, you really do know how to give a girl the five-star treatment!' she said, waspishly. 'And where do we dine?'

'Where do you suppose?'

'In the car?'

'Full marks,' I said. 'We treat ourselves to a drive-through burger, fries and giant diet Coke, and eat and drink while we're serenaded by music on the car's radio. Then we sleep in two-hour shifts; something like that. Don't I spoil you?'

'And all for what? Don't answer, Mike: *I'll* tell *you*. Just so we can both get suspended and ultimately demoted as soon as the brass find out where we are and what we've been up to, unknown to them.'

'Only if we fail,' I persisted, stubborn as ever. 'Anyhow, we're way beyond the rubicon in that respect. In for a penny, in for a pound.'

'No, Mike, in for a *pounding*,' she

predicted, with a withering glare.

We hired a medium-sized Chrysler from Hertz. When you're into surveillance mode, everything should be understated. Nothing flashy, nothing out of the ordinary, nothing that attracts. You dress down, not up, unless you're going to the Mayor's Ball, of course. Whatever the scene and situation, it's essential to blend in; to become part of the furniture or absorbed into the wallpaper, one of the crowd, a faceless commuter or bystander, always Mr and Mrs Average. When on surveillance duty, it's the one time when you strive for the status of non-entity.

★　★　★

I don't believe that either of us had more than a total of two hours' intermittent sleep. The smell from our takeaway meals seemed to intensify rather than disperse as the night wore on, despite our repeated efforts to cleanse the stale air in the car. I turned up the air-conditioning to maximum, but the odour from the fast food was slow to waft away; it clung to our clothes and seemed to have infiltrated our flesh.

Although the evening was mild, we were soon shivering as body heat was lost. There were no blankets in the car and, because it was summer, we didn't have top coats with us, so the only solution was to snuggle up, like a young couple who had to make do with a car as a love-nest. Neither of us could be called young, but we were lovers, so we were fifty per cent the real deal. The fact that we weren't posing with our affection gave legitimacy and conviction to our cover. Genuine lovers give out a scent, other than perfume and aftershave, and huddled together in a car was a natural sight at night. Some passers-by sniggered or shouted obscenities, but most had seen it all before and were too consumed by their own affairs to bother with us. The worst part of these surveillances was the boredom. Time seemed motionless. Mesmerized by the digital clock on the dash, I counted every second for hours and I really began to fear that morning would never come, that we had been plunged into eternal darkness, with the fire of the sun extinguished. Perhaps this was the beginning of the end of the world; God had flicked the switch, but had forgotten to turn off the lights of Manhattan.

Planes droned overhead on their final approach to JFK and thundered on take-off. By 3 a.m., the night-life in this residential neighbourhood had been reduced to a few stragglers; tipsy couples tottering barefooted, the women carrying their shoes. Bursts of spasmodic laughter competed with the screaming of fighting tom cats. Bats dive-bombed in the jaundiced glow of the street-lamps. Silhouettes cavorted in bed-room windows just before lights popped out. An owl, out of sight, hooted in one of the trees. The final curtain-call came late, only an hour or so before the stage was set for the first performance of the new day. There was little time lag between the late-to-bed and the early-to-rise.

Almost imperceptibly to begin with, the black shell of night began to crack. White slivers appeared first, then the yolk. The birth of the new day was over within an hour. The rush hour would be the unpleasant afterbirth.

New York City was waking up fast. A few people were already on the run; suited and shaven; hair blown, make-up applied, all groomed for the fray. Some jogged before their *real* day began.

Sarah unfurled and yawned. 'I'm cold and hungry,' she complained.

Before I could reply, a yellow cab cruised past us, slowing down, before stopping outside Tina's home.

Simultaneously, we both slipped on shades and sank low into our seats, so that we were partially hidden from the taxi.

Within a couple of minutes, Laura emerged, clad in jeans, white blouse, a caramel-coloured leather jacket and sneakers. She was carrying an overnight bag, slung over her shoulder. The bag wasn't big enough for an overcoat or many clothes, so she wasn't going into a cold climate.

Laura jumped into the rear of the cab, taking the bag inside with her.

Sarah was now as awake and alert as if she'd just stepped from under a cold shower.

'OK, we're on the move,' I said.

Game on.

16

Within a few minutes it was apparent that Laura was heading for JFK. Traffic was building, but we were an hour or more ahead of gridlock.

'What do we do with our rental car when we get to the airport?' said Sarah. 'Have you given that a thought?'

I hadn't. I saw the point she was making. Laura might have only a few minutes to catch her flight. The formalities involved with returning a hire car could take up to half an hour, especially if the company was busy. Laura might well have been checked in and passed through Passport Control before we were on our way from the car-rental lot.

'You see what I'm saying, Mike; we might lose her completely and never know which flight she boarded,' Sarah pressed her point, unnecessarily.

'We'll just have to dump the damned thing,' I said, seeing no alternative.

'It'll be towed within five minutes.'

'Great! The towers will do the job for us of returning the car.'

'Unless they reckon it's a booby trap and

blow it up. How irresponsible is that for a pair of Scotland Yard officers, one as senior as you?'

'Cometh the hour, cometh extreme measures!'

Before she could respond we were riding the ramp towards the drop-off zone for Departures. I pulled into the kerb about fifty metres behind Laura's cab. She hopped out, paid the fare, and hurried into the airport, without as much as a fleeting glance our way.

'OK, let's go,' I said. 'We don't want to get too close, but, equally, we mustn't fall too far behind.'

All the way along the concourse were check-in counters, with lines of people hauling their baggage, having passed the point where trolleys had to be abandoned. There were also hundreds of people milling around apparently aimlessly, as if not knowing where they were going, except in circles. Each airline had its own colony of counters. However, some of the smaller airlines had only one or two check-ins.

'Can you see her?' I said.

'Not a chance.'

'OK, let's take her at face value,' I suggested.

'And what, exactly, does that mean?'

'We look for Bahamas Airways.'

Sod's Law kicked in. Bahamas Airways had only one check-in desk, and that was at the far end of the concourse. While slicing our way through the queues and dodging the crowd of drifters, we had to keep our eyes peeled for Laura, in case she was preparing to check in with another airline for a destination somewhere other than the Bahamas.

'Got her!' Sarah suddenly exclaimed, stopping and putting out an arm to restrain me from going further.

'Where?'

'Right ahead. In the queue at the Bahamas Airways check-in desk. She's six from the front.'

'So she was telling the truth, not laying a false trail,' I said. By now I also had her in my sights. She had a ticket and passport in her hand and was pushing along her bag with a foot as she shuffled forward. I steered Sarah to the nearest monitor on which all departure times and destinations of flights were listed.

'Eleven a.m. to Nassau,' I read aloud from the screen.

'That means it should be boarding in about half an hour,' said Sarah, doing a quick mental calculation.

Simultaneously, we both looked for the Bahamas Airways ticket desk.

'Over there!' declared Sarah, pointing to a

small kiosk, wedged between two minor car-rental companies and a currency-changing outlet, towards the rear of the concourse.

Luckily, there was no queue at the kiosk, which could have been a good or bad indication for us.

'Have you any availability on your 11 a.m. service to Nassau?' I said to the smartly attired female ticketing-agent, adopting the parlance of the airline industry.

Not looking up, she tapped into her computer for a few seconds, before asking, 'How many travelling?' Now she did engage my eyes with a wonderful calypso smile, her teeth almost blinding me with their flawless luminescence.

'Two. Two adults.'

'OK, I can do that. Coach or Business?'

I hesitated and turned to Sarah.

'There are just two seats left in Business,' added the sales clerk.

Sarah could see the problem to which I was alluding with my expression and said to me quietly, 'It makes sense to take Coach.'

She was right again, of course. 'Yeah, Coach,' I said, passing over the *firm's* credit card and giving our names.

Within five minutes we were ticketed.

'Business class will be relatively small,' said Sarah, as we walked away. 'If we opted for

261

Business and Laura's also in that section, we couldn't possibly avoid her. And if she's in Coach, well . . . as long as she's not in the same row, we've a decent chance of staying incognito.'

'Because we'll be the last people she's expecting to encounter,' I said, continuing with Sarah's extrapolation. 'What really would be helpful would be to know what name she's using.'

A boy carrying a beach ball, who was clearly on his way to rejoin his parents or guardian in one of the queues, instantly gave me an idea.

'Hey,' I said to the boy.

He stopped and eyed me suspiciously, his alarm diluted, however, when he saw Sarah by my side.

'How would you like to earn twenty dollars?'

'How?' he said, edging closer, his face lighting up. I gauged his age about ten.

'You see that woman, second from the front in that line?' I said, pointing towards Laura's back.

'Yeah.'

'And you see the bag on the floor beside her with a label attached to the handle?'

'Yeah, I think so,' he said, hesitantly.

'Tell me what name's on the label and this

is yours,' I enticed him, producing a twenty-dollar bill from my wallet.

'She'll think I'm trying to steal the bag,' he vacillated, even though the bait was inflating his eyeballs.

'This is what you do: bounce your ball a couple of times, then lose control of it, so it rolls towards her, giving you an excuse for scrambling around on the floor near her feet.'

'To pick up my ball?'

'Exactly! Think you can do it?'

'That all you want me to do?'

'Nothing else, I promise.'

'And I get the twenty dollars just for *that?*'

'Just get me the name.'

'Done!' he said, and was gone.

'Let's hope we're in the clouds by the time his parents are demanding to know how he came by the twenty-dollar bill,' said Sarah, shaking her head in dismay.

We faced the opposite way to avoid being *made* should Laura follow the boy with her eyes after he'd completed the artifice.

We didn't have long to wait before the boy was in front of us again, now with a hand out and grinning broadly.

'Twenty dollars,' he said, very precocious and businesslike.

'Name first,' I said, proffering the bill, but not releasing it.

'Clapton. Laura Clapton.'

'You're a star,' I said, letting go of the reward.

'Good to do business with you!' said the boy, snatching the note and running off, his ball tucked under an arm.

Sarah laughed. 'He'll go far,' she said, admiringly.

'How about me? It was my bright idea.'

'For which, Inspector, you might make sergeant!'

★ ★ ★

We were among the last of the passengers to board. As we stepped into the Boeing 737, Business class was to our left, out of view. The senior flight attendant scrutinized our tickets, before saying, 'Your seats are in the very last row.' This, of course, meant that we had to run the gauntlet of all Coach passengers. People were still standing, cramming articles into the overhead lockers. Others were settling into their seats, fastening belts, reading about safety procedures, or just peering out of the porthole windows. We kept our heads lowered, but if Laura was in Coach and not distracted, we couldn't avoid being seen.

'Phew!' exclaimed Sarah, as we finally

reached the rear of the aircraft. 'I think we made it OK. She must be in Business. For once you made a winning bet!'

★ ★ ★

Two hours and fifty minutes later we landed in scorching Nassau.

We were in no hurry to disembark, so we allowed everyone else off the plane before us. There would be queues of passengers waiting to be processed at Immigration Control, so our idea was to ensure that Laura had passed through before we joined any of the lines. An even bigger danger-zone for us would be in the baggage-reclaim hall, where everyone from our flight would be buzzing like bees around one carousel.

'Let's hang back until we're confident she's gone beyond Immigration and Customs,' I said.

'Surely we'll lose her,' said Sarah, frowning.

'If she gets a cab, possibly . . . '

'But you don't think she will?'

'I reckon she'll be renting,' I predicted. 'That'll give us a chance to spot her at one of the car-rental outlets.'

'And how does that get us any further than knowing the owner of the vehicle she'll be driving?'

'When hiring a car, you're always asked for a contact address, such as the name of a hotel.'

'So how do you propose we get hold of that information?'

'That's where you come in,' I said, winking. She knew exactly what was expected of her. No briefing was necessary.

By the time we were out into the concourse, Laura was just leaving the Budget desk to board the rental firm's transfer bus to the car she'd been allocated.

'Go to work!' I said.

Sarah braced herself, grimaced at me, then rushed to the Budget desk, putting on a great act of being out of breath.

'Oh, my goodness, have I missed her?' I heard Sarah say to the young man in a white, short-sleeved shirt and dark-blue trousers.

'Who?' he said, obviously perplexed, his accent a cross between American (Deep South) and Caribbean.

'A friend I made on the flight from New York. Laura Clapton. We said we'd meet for dinner tonight. We got separated at baggage-claim. I know she was going to hire from you. She said to me, 'Whenever in Nassau, you *must* always rent from Budget. Trust me, they'll always take good care of you.''

'That's nice to hear, madam.'

266

'Well, anyhow, Laura seems a very discerning lady to me,' Sarah continued with her overload of flattery.

'Well, you've only just missed her.'

'Dammit! I don't suppose she told you the hotel where she has a reservation? We talked and talked about how we'd meet up, but forgot to exchange details about where we were staying. You must think us very stupid.'

'Not at all, madam. In fact, I think I can help you.'

'You can?'

'Yes, indeed. She did leave a contact address with us.'

'Really! I'd never have thought of that.'

He beamed and his chest swelled. 'Here we are: the Beachcomber, on Bay Street, bang in the centre of Nassau.'

'Oh, you're a darling!' Sarah gushed, planting a kiss on his cheek.

That's my girl! She should be on the stage earning real money.

★   ★   ★

'How was that?' she whispered, re-joining me outside the airport shop.

'No one can fake it better than you!'

Then we went to Hertz and hired one of their cars.

17

We got a room at the Paradise Inn, which was also located on Bay Street, near the Straw Market, but about half a mile from the Beach-comber.

The time had come to report our whereabouts to either Sharkey or Pomfrey; not a chore I relished, but it couldn't be deferred any longer.

'You've more bottle than I have, I'll grant you that,' said Sarah.

'I'd rather not do it, but if I delay much longer we'll find ourselves listed as missing persons,' I said. 'Imagine making the call then! 'Hi, Commander, thought I'd better let you know that we're fine and not at all missing. We're in a hotel, with a beach-front, in the Bahamas. Yes, that's what I said, the Bahamas. Just to prove it, I'll send a wish-you-were-here postcard.' No, I can't warm to that scenario. We must get in first.'

'No, Mike: *you* must get in first. This is all yours. I'm under your spell. You hypnotized me; that's my get-out. Although I can't deny that I'm here with you, nevertheless you're on your own.'

'You're loyalty's so heartening,' I said.

'I do sarcasm, you don't. Make the call, but allow me to get down to the bar first.'

'See you in ten, by the pool bar,' I said, as she opened the door.

'But will you be coming as Detective Inspector Lorenzo or plain Mr Lorenzo, that's the question.'

* * *

I chose to call Sharkey; a wise decision, by far the better of two evils. He was so speechless for the first couple of minutes that I had a free run.

At last he said, rather vapidly, 'You *are* joking?'

'Straight up,' I said, bloated with bravado, buoyed by his unexpected restraint. 'The bottom line is that we're near — so very, very close — to bagging Pope.'

'But . . . ' he started to say.

'We're closing in,' I cut him short.

'But why didn't you brief me?' he said, almost plaintively.

'Because I feared you'd put the kibosh on it,' I said, surprising him once more, this time with my candour.

'But for fucksake!' He was starting to regain consciousness, so it was time to cut and run.

'It's too long a story to go into now. The line's terrible this end and you're breaking up. Pass the update on to Pomfrey, won't you?'

I didn't hang around for an answer. Instead, I hung up with, 'I'll call you again tomorrow.'

'Hey, wait, listen . . . '

★   ★   ★

Sarah was already into her second whisky sour when I joined her at the pool bar, sheltered from the excoriating sun by a straw canopy.

'Well?' she said, removing the drinking straw from her mouth. 'What did you use to extinguish the fire in your ears?'

'No fire, not even smoke,' I said, hopping on to a stool beside her, shaking my head as the bartender approached.

'You're making this up as we go along, aren't you?' said Sarah, dismayed.

I understood exactly what she meant, but I made her spell it out.

'You don't have a game-plan. We've followed Laura to Nassau, but now what? If we go near her hotel, she's very likely to spot us. But if we don't get a handle on her, we'll have no idea what she's up to. If she's supposed to lead us to Pope, how can that

270

happen if we're not privy to her movements?'

'You're right,' I said.

'About what?' she retorted, argumentatively. 'I asked two questions.'

'I *am* making it up as we go along. I *don't* have a game-plan.' These admissions drew the steam from her.

She lowered her shades almost to the tip of her nose and gave me an old-fashioned look over the frames, eyeballs dilated. 'I think I prefer you brash and bullish to meek and conciliatory,' she said.

'We still don't even know what Pope looks like,' I said, keeping on track.

'Let's face it, Mike, we don't know *anything*.'

'What the hell is Pope doing here?' I said, more to myself than to Sarah, my gaze into space sightless.

'I could think of worse places to be dumped in disgrace,' said Sarah.

'I know all that, but what's his mission?'

'Maybe there isn't one.'

'You mean he's been banished here?' I said, now turning to face Sarah again.

'As good a place as any if you just wanted him plucked out of circulation and put into cold storage for a few months.'

'Hardly *cold storage*,' I said, smiling and dabbing sweat from my forehead. 'Instinct tells me there's more to it than using these islands as a hiding place.'

'Does the CIA have a bureau here?' said Sarah, squinting.

'Not that I've heard, but who knows?'

'So, there's no official outpost. His base could be a hotel room, same as us, same as Laura,' said Sarah.

'There's plenty of legitimate reasons for his being here,' I said.

'Such as?'

'The Mafia got a foothold in the Bahamas in the 1960s.'

'What on earth is there here for them?' said Sarah, frowning. 'Apart from a great holiday.'

'Plenty. Big-time gambling in the casinos. Ideal for them to skim profits and launder dirty money. They've also been using the outer islands as staging posts in the trafficking of drugs — heroin and cocaine — then flooding the US underground market, through Miami and Fort Lauderdale.'

'But Laura will know his whereabouts,' said Sarah, after a moment's cogitation.

'Oh, yes, she'll know. She'll know exactly where he is, even if not thoroughly *au fait* with his assignment.'

'So what's *her* plan?'

'That's another million-dollar question, Sarah.'

'We've come all this way and yet we're still

at an impasse. We're no further forward than when we left Oxford.'

'That's selling us a wee bit short,' I suggested.

'Well, how do we keep tabs on Laura if we can't do a surveillance job on her?'

'We get someone who can.'

'We can't go to the cops for help. We're not supposed to be here. We're a pair of long-haul truants, at best.'

'There must be gumshoes here,' I said. 'We can repeat the LA drill.'

'You reckon?' she said, sucking up the whisky sediment from her frosted tumbler.

'Got to be. Haven't you heard of the Bay Street Boys?'

'No,' she said, quizzically. 'We're on Bay Street now, aren't we?'

'That's right and this is where all the action is.'

'Yeah, I can see it all! Plenty of action drinking poolside and getting lethal melanomas.'

'The Bay Street Boys are wheeler-dealers. Big-time.'

'You're kidding?' said Sarah, seriously doubtful.

'For decades, the Bahamas has been an offshore haven for banking, insurance, real estate and tax avoidance; a colony of brass plates. There are companies trading in millions of dollars daily here. Banking millions, too. But the office on Bay Street may consist of nothing more than a brass plate on the door, an answer-machine, a mail-box and one employee. Just a front.'

'Like the Caymans?' said Sarah.

'Except the Bahamas was way ahead of the Caymans. There's a lot of money here, apart from that brought in by high-roller tourists. Massive colonial properties, too. Gin palaces on the water and yachts for billionaires. Along with the fast-living set are racy women.'

'Just the place for you, then.'

'On my salary? You're kidding!'

'Aren't we straying?' she said.

'Not my fault,' I said, defensively. 'I was going to explain that where there's so much moolah, sleazy commercial skulduggery and bed-hopping, there's bound to be a lucrative trade for professional snoops.'

'OK, so how do we go about finding one? I don't suppose they have anything like Yellow Pages here.'

'No idea, but they have two local newspapers, morning and evening.'

'And all newspapers carry Classified ads,' said Sarah, following my drift.

'So let's spend money in the shop in the lobby.'

We slid from our stools in a synchronized departure from the bar.

★   ★   ★

After buying a copy of the broadsheet *Nassau Tribune*, we parked ourselves on a leather settee in the cool, air-conditioned lobby to flick through the pages towards the Classified section at the tail-end of the publication.

Huddled together, scrolling down the columns with our fingers, we quickly came to the insertions under the 'Personal Services' heading.

'How about this one?' said Sarah.

I focused on the ad where her finger had stopped. *Female ex-Miami police officer, equipped to tackle almost any assignment. Has worked Vice, Narcotics and Homicide. Competitive rates. Anything considered. Tracing missing persons a speciality. So, too, checking out matrimonial and partnership infidelity. Also industrial espionage. Not an agency. Operates as Lone Ranger.* A mobile number was given, followed, in brackets, by *Day and night, 24 hours.*

'Worth a try,' I said.

We went to our room to make the call in private.

I thought I was about to be diverted to

275

voicemail, when the PI answered. 'Hold on, please, while I pull over.'

I could hear the thump of traffic in the background, which made me guess that she was driving a convertible. In a saloon, in this heat and humidity, the islanders drove with the air-conditioning on max and all windows closed. Open windows negated the cooling system.

'OK, I can talk now, please go ahead.' There was a South American or Caribbean cadence to her voice, leading me to speculate that she could well be second-generation Cuban American. A professional voice, direct manner, but very pleasant and articulate. With one sentence, she had made a good first impression, reminding me of my father's favourite maxim: *You never get a second chance to make a first impression.*

I decided to be equally direct. 'My name's Michael Lorenzo and I'm looking to hire someone like yourself.'

'You're English?'

'Correct.' *Some detective!*

'What's the nature of the job?'

'Surveillance.'

'On a person, persons, or a company?'

'A person.'

'Man or woman?'

'Woman.'

'She your wife, ex-spouse, mistress, or daughter?'

'None of those.'

I wasn't surprised by the elongated pause, before, 'Are you a resident of these islands?'

'No.'

'OK, why me?'

'First name to catch my eye in the local evening newspaper.'

'What about it appealed *especially*?'

'The fact that you're an ex-Miami cop.'

Flattery could be relied upon as a dependable tool.

'How long do you envisage this job taking?'

'As long as it takes.'

'Around the clock?'

'From the moment she's on the move in the morning until *she's* tucked up in bed with the light out, but not necessarily *around the clock*.'

'Are you hoping for snoopy bedroom stuff? Porno shots?'

'Nothing like that.'

'Voice recordings?'

'Maybe.'

'Long-range pics?'

'Always useful.'

'Where you staying?'

'Paradise Inn,' adding, 'I'm not alone.'

Now she hesitated and I knew why.

'It's OK, my companion's female. We're a couple.'

I sensed the evaporation of tension.

'You at your hotel now?'

'We are.'

'OK, I can be with you in fifteen.'

'Fine. We'll be in the lobby. How shall we recognize you?'

'You won't. I'll ID you. Give me a description.'

'Tall, dark, handsome and irresistible.'

'OK, you're short, fat, bald and ugly. Can't be missed.'

She had a quirky style and was winning me over rapidly. 'We'll be sitting on one of the couches, a copy of the *Nassau Tribune* spread on the table in front of us.'

'Less conspicuous than riding a pink elephant, I guess,' she said, deadpan. 'See you in fifteen. Oh, one last thing: I'd be obliged if you had a beer set up for me. I'm parched.'

'Done,' I said, but she was already gone.

'Sounds like you two are made for one another,' said Sarah, feigning jealousy. 'Mind you, she'll soon change her mind when she sees she was right: short, fat, bald and ugly!'

I kissed her on the cheek. 'Bless you!' I said, sorely. 'I didn't realize she was talking loudly enough for you to overhear. Come, let's bag ourselves a seat in the lobby.'

* * *

A waiter had only just deposited a Budweiser on the table in front of us when a voice directly behind me said, 'Mr Lorenzo?'

We both turned simultaneously to find ourselves looking at a brown-skinned blonde, about five-six tall and stunningly attractive; undoubtedly of Cuban heritage. Her eyes were shielded by large, reflector shades. She had the lips of a pugilist, highlighted with blood-red lipstick. Bulging breasts stretched a silky, cream top that was buttoned down the front. Her legs were encased in narrow-fitting, pale-blue designer jeans. Rawhide, pointed-toe cowboy boots completed the ranch-style picture.

'Carla Josez,' she said, offering a hand with long, artificial nails that had been painted the same colour as her lips. 'Don't take this as an insult, but, at this moment, I'm more pleased to see that beer than you two.'

'Some sales pitch!' I said, shooting her with a smile that was supposed to be read as, *Pleased to meet you, too!*

Carla took a long draw on the beer from the bottle before shaking Sarah's hand. We were the only people sitting in the lobby, which was busy, mainly with residents passing through, collecting or depositing room keys at

Reception or checking in and out. No one was taking any notice of us; not even the white-jacketed porters and waiters.

'So,' said Carla, 'what's the story?'

'As I said on the phone, it's a surveillance job on a woman: American Caucasian, age mid-forties, travelling alone, booked into the Beachcomber.'

'I assume you have a photo for me to work from?'

'No, but I can give you a graphic description and the name she's travelling under.'

Carla lowered her shades to impale me with enlarged and very expressive walnut eyes. 'You mean the name she's using is false?'

'Yes, but that's not the issue here.'

'Maybe not for you, but it could be for me.'

'Take my word for it,' I said, refusing to be drawn further. I had no intention of revealing that Laura was CIA and so too the person we were hoping she'd lead us to. No PI who valued his/her life would relish tangling with the CIA; anyone crazy enough to do so would treble the fee, calling it 'extreme danger money'.

Carla wasn't completely won over, but she shelved that line of questioning, at least for the time being. 'So, basically, you just want her followed?'

'We need to know about all men she meets,

plus photos of the meetings.'

'Nothing else?'

'Just locations.'

'So timewise it's open-ended.'

'Yes, but I can't see it running longer than two or three days.'

'Is there any chance of my being subpoenaed for a court appearance some place?'

'No.'

'Definitely no?'

'Rest assured, *definitely no*.'

'OK, a thousand Bahamian dollars up front as a retainer, five hundred dollars a day fee, plus expenses.'

'You're expensive,' I observed.

'I'm worth it.'

'How did I know you'd say that?'

'Because you've already assessed how good I am. My charges are commensurate with the workload and time involved. To do this job to your specifications, it would be impossible to combine it with other assignments. So you're paying for exclusivity.'

Case proved. Fee justified.

'A deal,' I said. 'I assume it's acceptable to you for payment with plastic?'

'Anything except cheques. Plastic has the advantage of being a universal currency.'

Carla had credit-card machinery with her and after the transaction had been sanctioned, she said, 'There's something I have to ask you. When I say *have to*, I mean for my own peace of mind, though there are many people in my trade who wouldn't be so fussy.'

'Fire away,' I said, making Sarah wince.

'If I come good for you, is there any prospect of the fruits of my labour being used unlawfully?'

'No chance,' I said.

'You may be lying, but I've asked the question and your answer enables me to go ahead with the commission, reasonably satisfied that I'm not getting involved in something I might live to regret. I have principles which I adhere to unyieldingly. Give me your mobile number.'

As she wrote down the digits, she said, 'This is the best way for me to keep in touch with you. The moment I have something positive to report or need further instructions in a hurry, I'll call, OK?'

'OK,' I confirmed.

'Any night-time deadline?'

'No. If something happens middle of the night that you reckon is worth reporting, call me.'

I left the description of Laura *Clapton* to Sarah, who had a unique ability to graphically sketch personality, as well as physical features, so succinctly with words.

'Brilliant!' said Carla, when Sarah had finished. She downed the remains of her Budweiser, rose, shook hands businesslike with us both, promised to make contact the moment she had any news, and disappeared into the early sunset. I was soon to discover that in the Bahamas the sun went down like a guillotine. There was no red and smouldering dying embers of the day; no seamless overlap. Daylight was decapitated; sudden death. Blackout.

'I think our Carla knows a thing or two about your proverb,' Sarah said, quietly, squeezing my hand. 'She realized that the first impression was the only one she was going to get a chance to make.'

18

We heard nothing from Carla for thirty-six hours. The same cannot be said of Sharkey or Pomfrey. Suffice it to say I stonewalled very badly. The blitz of calls ended with Pomfrey decreeing, 'You have forty-eight hours to wrap up whatever the hell you're *allegedly* packaging and be on a plane for London — or else!' I didn't ask for him to decode what 'or else' translated into.

Carla didn't call; she arrived, without warning, brimful of confidence.

Sarah and I were in the restaurant having breakfast when she swaggered in, photographic eyes snapping the scene. She located us within a single frame.

'I've made progress,' she said, hoisting her briefcase from the floor on to the table. 'Well, I think it's progress, but you two will have to be the judge of that.' She snapped open the briefcase and extracted a buff folder.

Sarah and I stopped eating.

'We have an interesting situation,' said Carla, slowly rolling her head and eyes. 'It didn't take me long to hook on to the target. What quickly became evident was that while I shadowed her, she was busy following someone else.'

'Who?' I said, suppressing excitement.

'A guy.'

'Have you managed to ID him?' said Sarah, impatiently.

'Sure. Dickie Lambert. US citizen.'

'Got any pics?' I asked.

'Naturally.' She opened the folder, producing photocopies that she'd obviously printed from her computer. Some of the shots were of Laura, others were of *Dickie Lambert*, who we knew must be Richard Pope.

'Did Lambert *make* her?' I said.

'No. This Laura is good. Very professional. *Too* professional.' Her eyes had become a little jumpy, shuttling between the two of us.

'Where did Laura latch on to him?' I asked.

'As he came out of an office on Bay Street, not far from here, further west, though.'

'Nearer the Beachcomber, where Laura's booked in?' I suggested.

'No more than two hundred yards away, yeah.'

'What kind of office?' said Sarah, squinting inquisitively.

'A trading company.'

'Trading in *what*?' I said.

'Imports and exports; well, that's what it says on the brass.'

'But what products?' I pressed, frustration pluming.

'Doesn't say. It's probably just a front for a scam; most of the companies here aren't legit. Could easily be a drug-trafficking outfit.'

'What's the name of the company?' Sarah enquired.

Carla referred to her file. 'Clint, Wood and East, Inc.'

'Not very clever,' I said. 'Switch the last two words, apart from Inc, and you have Clint Eastwood.'

'Gunslinger,' observed Carla, almost indifferently.

'More likely *gunslingers*, plural,' said Sarah.

Carla simply shrugged. 'Nothing too unusual about that here.'

'Where did he go?' I said.

'A couple of bars. Met a woman. Someone I recognized, but I don't know her by name, but she's a secretary in the office of one of the island's politicians. They exchanged envelopes.'

'You get pics of that?'

'Of course.' She patted the folder.

'How long did the meet last?' Sarah was anxious to know.

Carla looked up at the rotating colonial fan as she pondered the question. 'About ten or fifteen minutes. Time for a quick drink and some earnest, furtive talk.'

'Do you think he gave her money, a bribe?' I said.

'Listen, I deal in facts. I'm an ex-cop, right. I saw envelopes exchanged. I don't have X-ray eyes. I don't speculate. My thoughts on what might have been in the envelopes count for nought.'

I liked her answer because it endorsed the veracity of her report; she wasn't one for histrionics or embroidery.

'What next?'

'They shook hands and separated.'

'So it was a business meeting?' I said, posing another question. 'They weren't socializing? They were there for a transaction?'

'That's the way it looked.'

'Where was Laura all this time?' Sarah wondered aloud.

'Out of their direct line of vision, face half-shielded with large shades and head covered with a floppy hat.'

'Did she leave when they did?' I said.

'Yeah, she followed the guy.'

'That figures,' said Sarah.

'And you stayed on her?' I quizzed.

'Naturally. That's my brief, isn't it?'

'Of course,' I concurred. 'This must have been something of a procession; you on Laura's tail and she on his.'

'That's exactly how it was.' She wasn't

amused. In fact, I sensed she was becoming pissed off with my pedantry.

Carla took out the pics and handed them round, as if dealing playing cards. In appearance, Pope bore a close resemblance to his father, of whom there were many photographs on the internet, plus a detailed Wikipedia biography.

'Very distinguished,' murmured Sarah, but without admiration.

'And doesn't he know it!' sneered Carla. 'All the characteristics of a smooth viper. Just look at those reptilian eyes.'

I took no part in this particular assassination. Instead, I tried to visualize him in his rowing days at Oxford. He certainly had the physique, though much of his muscle had degenerated into flab. He hadn't lost much hair, but it was now the colour of tinsel. All oarsmen needed gargantuan hands — *all the bigger to strangle you with* — and Pope was no exception. His head was boulder-shaped and his slightly hooded eyes were set deeply in pendulous flesh. In a couple of shots, he was flashing teeth that seemed to have been fastidiously preserved. As for his clothes, he was dressed to be absorbed in any wallpaper of the Bahamas: garish, short-sleeved shirt, blue silk slacks and white brothel-creeper shoes.

'Did Laura return to her hotel?' I asked, moving on.

'Not right away. First, she drove to the quay to a boat-hiring business.'

'What sort of boats?'

'Small fishing craft and speedboats. She was there about twenty minutes and came away with what looked like a brochure or tariff. Then she drove to the hotel.'

'And didn't surface again?'

'Not out the front; not by car.'

'Is there any other way of leaving the hotel?' Sarah quizzed.

'Yes, but only on foot. She could walk through the pool area to the beach, then go either way, east or west. But she was in her room at 10p.m.'

'How can you be sure of that?' I said.

'Because I called the hotel from my car on my mobile and asked to be put through to her room She answered.'

'And you hung up?' said Sarah.

'Not without speaking because to have just killed the call might have aroused her suspicions. I said, 'Sorry, I must have the wrong room. I'm calling my mother and I can tell you're not her age.''

'So you got an early night?' I said.

'No. I hung around in the hotel parking lot until midnight just in case she did emerge to join the night-owls.'

'But she didn't?'

'No. Perhaps she wanted a good night's sleep to be fresh for a fishing trip today.'

That set me thinking.

'Is that it?' said Sarah.

'For now. You can keep that report and the pics; I have copies. I'd better get back on the beat and try to catch up with her. My bet is she'll already be out of her hotel, but this is a small town; no place to hide. As long as she's on the move by car, I should be able to sniff her out without too much trouble.'

'You're doing a good job,' I said, affably.

'Just what are you expecting from this?' Carla said, puzzled. 'You seem to be investing a lot of money for a very mundane, limited return. Not that I'm complaining.'

'I can't tell you anything more, Carla, but suffice it to say you're getting us everything we want. But now's the time for a change of focus.'

Carla caught on immediately. 'You want me to concentrate on the guy, Dickie Lambert?'

'Most importantly, we need instant warning should he seem to be preparing to leave the island,' I said.

'Are you cops?' Carla said, suddenly, her eyes jumping back and forth between me and Sarah.

'Now what gave you that idea?' I said, stalling.
'So you are!'

'I didn't say that,' I said, without conviction.

'Oh, but you did! I was a cop, remember; a damned good one, too, even though I say so myself. I was trained to translate evasive answers. What I haven't figured out yet is who's the *real* target.'

'Just keep the meter running and pocket the money,' I implored. 'You're doing fine.'

'Does it matter who or what we are?' Sarah butted in.

Carla shrugged again, a mannerism of hers that I was beginning to recognize. 'Could do. I don't knowingly take commissions from gangsters.'

'And would you classify cops as gangsters?' I said, teasingly.

'Oh, yeah, quite easily! Especially where I come from.' Getting up, she added, 'OK, I don't know what's going on, but I'll play along for the time being. But, be warned, if I smell a rat . . . '

'Oh, you'll smell a rat, all right, Carla, but it won't emanate from present company, believe me,' I said.

A little happier now, Carla made off with her briefcase, treating us to an over-the-shoulder, irreverent wave. Like Sarah, she had style.

Just after lunch I took a call on my mobile from Carla. She was breathless now, adrenaline making her voice hoarse.

'Things are developing,' she said. 'Fast. Nasty. I'm on the road. Trailing a car. You need to play catch-up; quick as you can. I'll try to give you directions that you can follow easily. I'm out of my comfort zone, losing the plot.'

'Whose car are you pursuing?' I said.

Sarah's ears twitched like those of a rabbit.

'His. But they're together.'

'*They?*' I said, perplexed.

'*Lambert* and Laura.'

Carla was losing me. 'What am I missing?' I said.

'I'll explain as soon as you're rolling. Keep your phone open. The vibes are bad here. Very, veree bad.'

'Handing you over to Sarah,' I said.

We were in the lobby. Sarah was pulling faces, mutely asking for the storyline.

'Let's go,' I urged, as Sarah took my cell-phone.

By now we were running through the parking lot, wringing wet as if under a steaming shower. Out of the shade, the temperature was at least forty degrees centigrade. Not a cloud between Nassau and Miami, ninety miles to the east. The only breeze came from the vortex whipped up by our own exertions. By the time we reached our Oldsmobile, we were both hyperventilating.

'We're about to roll,' Sarah spoke into the phone as I gunned the engine. 'Which way should we turn on to Bay Street?'

'Right,' said Carla. 'Hug the coastal road. Don't peel off towards the airport. Keep the ocean in sight on your right.'

Sarah relayed instructions to me, saying to Carla, 'Where are you?'

'About five minutes ahead of you. *Lambert's* at the wheel of the car — with a gun pressed to the back of his head. Laura's gun.'

Sarah passed this information to me dispassionately, staccato-style. She was always at her cool, professional best in hairy situations.

'I've got to alert the local cops,' said Carla. 'We can't play this solo.'

I agreed. The show had to be opened up. It was imperative that we stayed on the right side of the law.

'Ask her where she reckons they're heading?' I instructed Sarah.

Carla's answer was what I feared: 'No idea.'

'How did this begin?' Sarah asked.

'She was waiting for him as he emerged unsuspectingly from his office,' said Carla.

'He opened the driver's door of his car, got in, and as he was sticking the key in the ignition, she jumped in the rear. She must have already drawn the gun because, as he swung round, he found himself staring down that scary little black hole.'

'Where were you?' said Sarah.

'Sitting in my parked car across the road, about a hundred yards away, binoculars on them.'

'No other witnesses?' said Sarah.

'No one else around close enough. She was talking in the car, obviously reading him the riot act. He turned away from her, so he was facing ahead. Then they were wheeling, taking it nice and steady.'

Before Sarah could pop any more questions, Carla said excitedly, 'They're pulling off the road.'

'How far are you behind?' Said Sarah.

'Two hundred yards. I've slowed. I mustn't get too close yet. I'm stopping. They're jumping ship. I'm going the rest of the way on foot. You'll see my car at the side of the road. I'm disconnecting now to call the cavalry.'

Sarah had treated me to a non-stop running commentary.

'This is getting out of hand,' she said.

The road was not made for rallying. It was narrow and circuitous, with holes like craters.

Even so, I kept my foot flat on the pump, as if I was trying out for a place in a Formula One racing team. We were kicking up dust as if crossing the Sahara. We sped past large, colonial-fashioned houses among palms and pines to our right, with their own ocean-fronts and private marinas. Through the trees we caught glimpses of the endless white sand.

As we careened round a tight right-handed bend, leaning into the tilt, with Sarah almost propelled on to my lap, we spotted Carla's abandoned car just ahead. I hit the brake pedal just as hard as I'd been accelerating, subjecting our vehicle to the severest possible stress as we went into a skidding tailspin before shuddering to a halt, our nostrils assaulted by the overpowering smell of burning rubber.

Sarah was first out of the car, but I soon caught up.

'This way,' she said, leading me into a clearing that led to a narrow, stony track. 'They must have gone this way. The sea can't be far away.'

The path was sinuous and gloomy because little sunlight was able to filter through the roof of leaves and branches. We didn't have far to go. After two bends, we were suddenly on sand with the beach directly ahead.

Carla was standing on the beach with

binoculars pressed to her eyes. She heard our running footsteps and turned, but only briefly.

'Where are they?' I said, as we joined Carla, who pointed out to sea.

A speedboat was cutting a soapy swath through the transparent, turquoise southern Atlantic, a frothy trail in its wake.

'The boat was just throttling away from that jetty when I got here,' said Carla. '*Lambert* at the controls, Laura behind him.'

'Still with the gun to his head?' I asked.

'Oh, yeah. The brain-mincing Magnum was still in her hand; still tickling the hairs of his neck.'

I looked at the tiny jetty; no other boat was moored there. Neither did the jetty appear to belong to any property; there was no house nearby, as far as I could see.

'Where do you suppose they're going?' I said.

Carla shrugged, keeping her US Army-issue binoculars pinned on the speedboat. 'Apparently not Paradise Island, which is to our right. They're arcing left, heading sort of northwest.'

'Towards Florida?' Sarah suggested.

'That direction, yes, but they'll never make it in *that* thing. Couldn't possibly carry enough gas.'

Just then the throttle cut back, with the speedboat about a half-mile from shore.

'They might have run out of juice already,' Carla surmised, wishfully. 'No power at all now. They're drifting. Oh, shit!'

'What now?' I demanded, cogently, not able to follow the action without binoculars.

'She's drawn a knife.'

'A knife!' I intoned, mystified. 'What about the gun?'

'She's transferred the gun to her left hand. The knife's in her right hand, Jesus! I don't get any of this. No sense in this at all. How many weapons does she need?' The question was rhetorical. 'It's a flick-knife; gangland weapon.' Then, as an aside, 'Where the hell are the cops? They should be here by now. Probably coming on skateboards!'

'What's the guy doing now?' I said.

'Filling his pants, I guess. She's edging towards him. He's backing off as much as he can, without toppling overboard. Now she's lashed out.'

'With the knife?' I said, eagerly.

'Yeah. She's cut him. On the hand. The hand he put up to shield his face. He's clasping his hand, trying to wrap a handkerchief around it.'

I didn't understand this at all. 'And what's *she* doing?'

'Seems to be just standing there, watching.'

'Not using the knife any more?' said Sarah.

'No, she's thrown it overboard. This is weird.'

Police-car sirens were wailing in the distance, still some way off.

'Do they have a fix on us?' I asked, alluding to the cops.

'They have a car reg,' said Carla. 'They'll find us soon enough.'

'Anything new happening on the boat?' I said.

'You bet! Now she's waving the gun in his face. He's shaking his head. I wish I could lip-read. Guessing, I'd say he's still pleading to be spared: *Please don't do it!*'

The sirens were much closer now; could be no further away than half a mile.

'Jeese!' exclaimed Carla. 'He's jumped!'

'Over the side?' I said, stupidly.

'Yeah. Fully clothed. Shirt, slacks, shoes. He's splashing around. He doesn't look much of a swimmer. But now she's tossed him a lifebelt! This is bizarre. She forces him over the side, then throws him a lifeline.' She turned to us distrustfully, her stare fierce and challenging, as if we must somehow be a party to this comic opera.

Now it was my turn to shrug helplessly.

Carla returned to her watching brief. 'She's

restarted the engine.'

'So it hadn't run out of fuel,' Sarah commented, needlessly.

Carla made no reply, instead saying. 'She's steering away from him. Abandoning him. Heading back to shore, this way. Now she's gotten rid of something else over the side. Could be a gun.'

I scratched my head, trying to fathom the significance of what I was being fed. 'What's *he* doing?'

'Holding on to the ring. Staying afloat. He should be OK. The ocean's as flat as a living-room carpet, even that far out. The cops can have a rescue launch out to him in no time at all.'

The speedboat, with Laura standing erect at the controls, wasn't speeding now. Behind us, the pounding footsteps on the stones announced the belated arrival of uniformed cops, led by a sergeant.

Carla handed me the binoculars while she spoke with the four officers. Out of the corner of an eye, I could see Carla jabbing a finger seawards, towards the spot where Pope, *Lambert* to her, had plunged into the water.

Brushing Carla aside, the sergeant marched to me, demanding, 'Gimme! Let me have a look.' Before I had a chance to react, he snatched the binoculars. Moments later, he said, 'I can see a speedboat, but that's all. The boat's making for here, it seems to me. Just one person on board, a woman. No man. No one out there in the water, as far as I can see.'

'Let me show you,' said Carla, retrieving her binoculars and pointing them towards the distant point where Pope had been clinging to a lifebelt. 'That's strange,' she muttered, after a moment of panning the area of her magnified focus. 'I've got the lifebelt in my sights, but . . .'

'Show me,' said the sergeant. 'Let me see.'

Carla returned the binoculars to the sergeant and helped guide his trajectory of vision so that he was focusing on the appropriate patch of water.

'OK, got it,' he said. 'Got the lifebelt. Nothing else, though.' He began scanning a wider area. 'No. Definitely no one in the water out there.'

'I *really* don't get it,' said Carla. 'He had a firm hold on the lifebelt. He was secure. No rough water. You can see what it's like. Calmer than in a teacup. All he had to do was wait.'

To his men, the sergeant said, 'I'm going to commandeer the speedboat. One of you come with me. I want the two staying behind to start taking statements. Bottom this out as quickly as possible. It's fishy. And all fish stink!'

The speedboat was just buffeting the jetty as the sergeant finished giving orders to his men.

'This your boat?' said the sergeant, as he hopped on to the craft's bow.

'No, it's rented,' said Laura, unperturbed, her eyes shooting instant recognition towards me and Sarah; no signals of surprise or alarm.

'I'm confiscating it,' the sergeant stated, peremptorily.

'Be my guest,' said Laura.

'Was there a man with you?'

'There was.'

'Where is he now?'

'Out there somewhere,' Laura said, temperately, peering towards the horizon, gesturing vaguely.

'How did he get in the ocean?'

'He jumped.'

'Why?'

'You'd better ask him.'

'You've a lot of explaining to do, lady.'

'Don't you think you should stop talking and go pull him out?'

Just before launching the speedboat, the sergeant called from his mobile for police launches to join the search for Pope.

For a moment the throaty roar of the speedboat's finely tuned engine was deafening; not until it was some two hundred yards from the shore was there any point in our trying to be heard.

Laura sidled up to me, smirking, to say, 'You took your time.'

'What's that supposed to mean?' I replied. She was playing with us, I could tell. I had a feeling that we were dancing to her tune, and not just today, though we weren't in step and she was almost disappointed with us.

'I knew you'd be here,' she said, as the two Bahamian cops looked on, bemused. 'I'm not talking about being at this particular spot. It was given that it wouldn't take you long to have me sussed; in fact, I was counting on it. As soon as you'd blown my cover and knew how I really earned my mortgage money, I figured you'd anticipate I'd find a way of going after that piece of shit. Although we worked for the same agency, it didn't make us colleagues. I owed him no loyalty. The Disciples worked for one man, but even they had a Judas among them. Well, *our* Judas is already in hell with the original, take my word for it. You reasoned I'd easily be able to find out where Pope had been posted. But did you really believe you could follow me without my knowing? If you did, that was rather arrogant of you, don't you think? I actually went out of my way to make it easy for you. I had to really work at being artless. In fact, I began to worry you'd miss the flight I boarded at JFK for Nassau.'

Switching to Carla, Laura said, 'I guess you're a PI *these two* have wasted money on?

Carla, hands on hips, shades pushed up to her head, assumed the combative posture you'd expect from a screen cowboy just before drawing a gun from its holster for a High Noon showdown. 'Is someone going to explain what's going on here; what I'm missing?'

'That's what *we* intend to find out,' interjected one of the cops, before Sarah or I had a chance to answer.

* * *

Two hours must have passed before the speedboat returned, by which time a flotilla of small boats, of all descriptions, had gathered in the area where the search had been concentrated.

The sergeant, now grim-faced, with his peaked cap pushed back and tilted upwards, came towards us along the jetty, while his acolyte tied up the boat.

'OK, we found him,' he said, hands gripping his hips, using his eyes as rapiers to aim at we four civilians. 'Forget what I just said, which was an exaggeration; a *gross* exaggeration. To be accurate, I should have said we recovered *bits* of him. One arm, a leg, part of a disembowelled torso, and a head detached from its neck.'

'Well, he was in one piece when he leapt over the side,' said Laura, not a shade of shock on her face, not a flicker of horror in her eyes or a tremor in her voice.

'Could he have got chewed up by the speedboat's high-powered motor?' said Sarah, lagging a little.

'Not a chance,' said the sergeant. 'There's no mystery about the cause of death. When a shark fancies a club sandwich, it is a messy eater. No table manners whatsoever.'

Sarah was the only one among us to blanch.

'From what you say, it seems like the shark spat out quite a bit of him, suggesting the beast had good taste!' said Laura.

19

The four of us were detained overnight in the Nassau Central Police Station. We were interviewed separately and kept in different cells, so it wasn't until the dust had settled and most issues had been sorted that we were able to compare notes.

As for my part, I recognized that now was not the time for further cloak-and-dagger mischief. Now was the moment for candour and co-operation; prevarication wasn't an option. I explained that I was a senior Scotland Yard detective. So, too, was Sarah, though not quite as senior.

'Prove it,' said my interviewer, a perfectly reasonable request from a dour Bahamian uniformed officer, in his mid-thirties, I'd say, who toyed with his polished baton on the desk as if itching to use it for something more than mere show.

So prove it I did.

Bushy eyebrows raised, he examined my police ID as if he had been forced to pick up dog poo with his bare hands.

'Could be a forgery,' he observed, as if inciting me to react disproportionately.

Naturally, I didn't bite. 'Of course it *could* be,' I replied. 'But it isn't. Check me out.'

'Oh, we shall,' he promised, digging deep for menace. 'I suppose you have a passport?'

I eased my passport from my jacket, which was folded haphazardly in my lap.

He journeyed through the pages like a slow reader with myopic eyesight, holding the document close to his humourless face.

Finally, he said, 'We'll keep this.'

'Your prerogative,' I said.

My compliance was clearly not to his liking. I sensed he was seeking confrontation, something he probably enjoyed. Especially with foreigners. And most especially with foreign cops whom he imagined as uppity, considering themselves superior, a charge to which I could honestly plead not guilty.

'OK,' he said, reclining in his chair, kicking his black-booted feet on to the desk and constructing a tent with his fingers, 'what's the story?' *What's the story?* seemed to be the cliché of the month in cop circles.

He made *story* sound as if he was asking for a fable.

For the next fifteen minutes, I regaled him with a synoptic version of our reason for being in Nassau; in a nutshell, we had information leading us to believe that a suspect for a series of murders and other serious crimes in the UK many years ago was in his country.

'So why didn't you liaise with us?'

A valid question; tricky too. One I'd prepared for but still hadn't come up with a response that would satisfy me if I'd been on the other side of the desk.

'I don't think you'll like the answer,' I said, trying a smile of camaraderie that bounced back like a worthless cheque.

'I'm sure I won't,' he agreed.

This was hard labour without gas and oxygen for pain relief.

'I didn't want to take the chance of a screw-up.' This he took as an insult, which at least demonstrated that he was smarter than I'd been taking him for. 'I'm not being rude,' I added, which was true, but wasn't something he wished to believe, so obviously he didn't. 'The more people and different forces who knew about the operation, the greater the chance of a leak or a cock-up; you know, treading on each other's toes or getting killed by *friendly* fire.'

'We don't have cock-ups,' he said. 'None of our fire is friendly. We run a tight ship. We don't have leaks.'

'You're very lucky, then,' I said. 'I envy you.' God! Thank heaven I wasn't a diplomat. I couldn't do this diplomacy dance every day for a living.

His next question concerned Carla. How did she fit into the jigsaw? When I told him, he was even more irked.

'So you thought a single private eye could do a better job than a whole team of professional Bahamian police officers?'

I was in more mire of my own making. 'As I said, I didn't want too many people involved,' I explained, weakly. 'I didn't want it going arse-up.'

'And *this* is what Scotland Yard calls getting it right?'

'Well, it seems after thirty years we finally got our man.'

'No, the shark did.'

Nice one! I thought, according credit where it was due.

More awkward than anything was trying to explain how Laura fitted into this imbroglio.

'So now we have the CIA!' he said, derisively. 'The private detective follows the CIA, who follows Richard Pope, though Carla has been told his name is Dickie Lambert, who also happens to be CIA. Do, please, correct me if I'm mistaken.'

'You're not mistaken,' I said. I would have been the first to admit that this saga sounded like a storyline of an old corny *Carry On* movie farce. However, it soon became apparent that CIA carried far more weight in the Bahamas than did Scotland Yard.

By midnight, the Bahamas' chief constable had taken charge, liaising closely with the islands' governor. Laura was soon the focal point. Carla, apparently, described exactly everything she'd witnessed from the time Pope was abducted.

Laura simply went into semi-denial. Yes, she did have a gun and forced Pope to drive to the jetty, where the speedboat was moored. She'd hired the boat over the phone from her hotel room, paying for it by credit card and asking for it to be left at the out-of-town mooring, just off the coastal road, where she'd collect it. Her intention, she said, was to 'scare the shit' out of Pope, so that he would confess to his crimes. She had made him drive to the moored speedboat and, at gunpoint, had compelled him to steer the high-powered craft into deep water. She denied having a knife and cutting Pope's hand.

In her statement, she said, 'Anyone who says I had a knife and used it on Pope is mistaken. How could they possibly be sure of what they saw from such a distance? I was trying to terrify the bastard into confessing. It's true I wanted him to fear I might blow off his head if he wasn't forthcoming, but I wouldn't have harmed him, not intentionally.

Instead, he panicked and dived overboard, reckoning on being able to swim ashore, but forgetting how far out we'd gone. I threw him a lifeline and left him to sort out his own salvation, confident he'd be rescued, even if he was dangling in the water a couple of hours.'

Of course there were as many holes in her story as a torpedoed battleship. For a start, she wasn't taping the conversation, so if Pope had confessed, how could she possibly prove that he'd come clean? CIA didn't make those kinds of elementary mistakes. And why had she disposed of the gun? 'Because it was no longer required?' she told her sceptical interviewing officer.

In the days I had been in the Bahamas, I had read stories in the *Nassau Tribune* of Tiger sharks spotted in considerable numbers off the beaches, in the shallows. Two swimmers had been attacked in one day; both were lucky and had escaped with relatively minor wounds. Lifeguards had warned tourists to stay out of the sea and stick to hotel pools until an 'all-clear' was given. The reason for Laura arming herself with a gun *and* a knife was suddenly so transparent to me. The gun forced Pope into compliance; the knife drew blood, which served as an open invitation to afternoon tea for all sharks in the neighbourhood. Laura didn't have to kill Pope because she knew that the natural world would do the job for her. Having him arrested would have been a pointless exercise; the CIA machinery would have gone into overdrive and Pope would have disappeared yet again — perhaps to behind a desk at HQ, where he would have been forever untouchable. The scales of justice in this case had been balanced by nature.

While we were detained, talks were going on between legal advisors to the Bahamas' chief constable and their counterparts in London and Washington.

At 9 a.m., without breakfast, a drink, or even the opportunity for a wash and brush-up, Sarah, Laura and myself were ushered from our holding cells into vehicles and driven, at speed, to the airport. Laura went in a blacked-out limo; Sarah and I slummed it in a bone-shaker van. We were handcuffed together and forbidden to communicate to one another. At the airport, we were kept in the van until Laura had been escorted on to a Washington-bound flight. As soon as that aircraft was on the runway, we were unshackled and led to a Miami flight that was already boarding. Tickets had been purchased on our behalf that would take us through to London, connecting in Miami that evening for Heathrow. Scotland Yard would be billed — something else for Commander Pomfrey to be thrilled about.

★   ★   ★

Next morning, when we landed at Heathrow around 8.40 a.m., two officers from the Metropolitan Police Commissioner's office were waiting to hurry us straight to the Yard.

Pomfrey was pacing. Pomfrey was popping indigestion tablets like a junkie. Pomfrey was red with rage. 'You've broken every rule in the book. You're mavericks who have lost your marbles. You not only went AWOL, but flitted around the world on Yard plastic, as if it were a magic carpet. Theoretically, you're guilty of misusing public money, in addition to a million other criminal and professional offences.'

'Something of an exaggeration,' I unwisely ventured.

'Zip it!' Pomfrey roared. Eyeballing Sarah, he said, 'I'm surprised at you.'

'Why, sir?'

'For allowing this unprincipled, irresponsible, undisciplined reprobate to lead you astray.'

'We're partners,' she said, stoutly.

'Parsnips, more like!' he fumed. 'Fucking

parsnip-heads! Thick and . . . and . . . ' He didn't know where he was going with this and that made him even more irascible. 'A disgrace! Both of you.'

We were slumped in chairs, while he promenaded. I had a two-day growth of beard and hadn't washed since I last shaved. I was also still dressed for Nassau. Fortunately, the weather was mild in London. On the overnight flight from Miami, I'd splashed on some aftershave that was provided in the toilets and at Heathrow I'd swilled my face with cold water, but still I considered myself a wreck of titanic proportions. By comparison, Sarah looked as if she'd just stepped out of a beauty salon following meticulous grooming. Nature could be very unfair.

One of Pomfrey's male brown-tongues sat muted in a corner, taking notes. I assumed a tape recorder wasn't being used so that all Pomfrey's expletives and banality wouldn't be recorded and a summary of the meeting could be outrageously edited.

'Well, what have you to say for yourselves?' he demanded, looking down at me.

'We closed a case that no one else could in three decades,' I replied, flatly. 'More kudos for the Yard.'

'Is that *all* you can say?'

In six little words Pomfrey had given a

313

remarkable insight into the psyche of the police hierarchy.

Sarah looked at me, I looked at her, and I really thought that we were both about to crease up; the only reason we didn't, I'm certain, is because we were both so bombed.

'Well, this *is* what's going to happen,' Pomfrey motored on, once more parading, silver buttons gleaming, starched white collar biting into his roseate neck, buffed black shoes reflecting the immaculate cut of his funereal-black uniform. 'Neither of you will make any statement to the media. In fact, when you vacate my office, you'll immediately commence two weeks' leave.

'I shall be issuing a statement to the effect that two Scotland Yard detectives have brought closure to a series of murders that terrorized the city of Oxford three decades ago. I shall further say that having been traced to the Bahamas, the guilty party died while attempting to escape; that he fell into the sea from a rented boat and was killed by a shark or sharks. The report will be as skeletal and sketchy as possible. Some 'papers doubtlessly will despatch reporters to the Bahamas to sniff around, to put meat on the bone, but they won't get far. The private dick you hired at an exorbitant daily rate has been warned she'll lose her licence and

Bahamian work permit should she utter a word, so she's silenced.

'The CIA wanted their agent back — the one of the two still living. She'll be grounded for the rest of her career, but not booted out, so I'm told. They don't want her mouthing to the media about any black ops she or Pope had been a part of, which could happen if charges were brought against her.

'The Bahamas police were pleased to see the back of the lot of you, something with which I can fully empathize. A foreign serial killer had gone to the sharks and the Bahamian authorities didn't relish a stand-off with the Americans. The Bahamas economy is tied like a joined twin to the US, so politics played well for all you lucky sods.

'Of course, the pair of you are finished with Oxford. When you return from leave, your futures will depend on me. We're not getting rid of you only because, as loose cannons, out of the fold, you'd be more of a headache than in and on a tight leash. Understood?'

The diatribe had been directed solely at me, not Sarah, so I answered for us both. 'Understood.'

'You're sure?'

Pomfrey wanted blood.

'Sure.'

'Out, then! On your way! Oh, one more

thing — a suggestion this time rather than an order.'

Makes a change, I thought, but said, 'Yes?'

'Get a bath and make yourself look like a member of the human race, even if you're not.'

★ ★ ★

Half an hour later, just as we were about to hop on a double-decker, Sharkey came through on my mobile. 'Brave man, Mike. Great job! Sometimes gambling does pay! Ignore the brass, but you'll always do that without any encouragement from me. Tina's been informed about the outcome and sends her thanks. She said what a coincidence that Pope should have met his end in the Bahamas at the same time that her partner was there on risk management business for her company! She has no idea that you and Sarah were there too. Let's keep it that way.' Before I could conjure up a suitable riposte, he was gone.

'Who was that?' said Sarah.

'Oh, nobody really,' I replied, abstractly. 'Just someone I once knew from what now seems a very distant past.'

Within five minutes of leaving Pomfrey we'd decided to take off for a few days away from the madding crowd. After packing a few

essentials, such as toothbrushes and condoms, we were undecided whether to train it
from Victoria to Brighton or Paddington to
Torquay, both towns on the south coast.

'Toss for it,' suggested Sarah.

'Heads Brighton, tails Torquay,' I said.

Sarah tossed, caught the coin, and flipped
it on to the back of her hand. 'Heads,' she
said.

'OK, Brighton it is,' I confirmed. 'I'll make
a reservation.'

I knew I ought to phone my estranged wife
and ask after the kids, but my brain was too
blitzed for any meaningful conversation and
most definitely far too fragile for mental
sparring.

That evening, having booked into a hotel
on the seafront, we dined from Room Service
and drowsily stretched out together on the
bed, channel-hopping by remote to see if we
could catch a soporific movie on TV.

We thought we had hit lucky, only to
discover that the film just beginning was *Jaws
IV*.

'No! No! No more sharks,' decreed Sarah,
snatching the remote from me and slaying the
beast with one touch of the red button, a trick
that had not been available to Richard Pope.

Sleep came easily, but, unfortunately, so
did the nightmares.

Other titles published by
The House of Ulverscroft:

AN INVISIBLE MURDER

Joyce Cato

When travelling cook Jenny Starling starts her new job at Avonsleigh Castle, she is thrilled. She envisions nothing more arduous than days spent preparing her beloved recipes. But when a fabulous bejewelled dagger, one of the castle's many art treasures, is used to murder a member of staff, the Lady of the House insists that Jenny help the police with their enquiries. But how was it done? The murder was committed in front of several impeccable witnesses, none of whom saw a thing. It seems the reluctant sleuth must once again discover the identity of the killer in their midst . . .

THE DOLL PRINCESS

Tom Benn

Manchester, July 1996, the month after the IRA bomb. The *Evening News* reports two murders. On the front page is a photograph of an heiress to an oil fortune, her body discovered in the basement of a block of flats . . . Buried in the later pages there's a fifty-word piece on the murder of a young prostitute. For Bane, it's the latter that hits hardest. Determined to find out what happened to his childhood sweetheart, it soon becomes clear that the two stories belong on the same page, as Bane immerses himself in a world of drugs, gun arsenals, human trafficking and a Manchester in decay . . .